CHRISTMAS SISTERS

SOUL SISTERS AT CEDAR MOUNTAIN LODGE

VIOLET HOWE   TAMMY L. GRACE   EV BISHOP
TESS THOMPSON   JUDITH KEIM

MADDIE KIRBY

AUTHOR VIOLET HOWE

"Even worse than Thanksgiving, think about Christmas! How on earth will she make it through Christmas?"

Maddie had just reached for the knob on the bathroom door when she heard the ladies enter the teachers' lounge, but she drew her hand back and clutched it to her chest when she realized they were discussing her.

"I have no idea. I have a hard-enough time with my family all being back East. I can't imagine what it would be like to lose your husband and your only child at the same time and then face your first holidays without them."

"And the poor woman had already lost her father to a heart attack a few months before the car accident," said Paula, the eighth-grade math teacher. "How much tragedy can one person take?"

"I couldn't believe she came back to school this year," said Joyce, the seventh-grade history teacher. "I don't think I could have."

"Maybe it's easier, you know? Focusing on work and staying busy."

"Yeah, maybe. Lord knows being a guidance counselor

keeps her busy, but you know while she's listening to everyone else's issues and problems all day, she has to be thinking that no one here—student or staff—has it as hard as she does."

Maddie held her breath as Paula's voice came closer to the bathroom door. She wished there was another exit so she could escape without them knowing she had overheard them. The last thing she wanted was an awkward confrontation with embarrassed apologies.

She breathed a sigh of relief when she heard the refrigerator door open and close, and then the microwave beeped and whirred into action as the ladies moved on to a discussion of Christmas shopping still to be done.

Maddie leaned her hip against the sink and crossed her arms, determined to remain hidden until they'd gone. She didn't begrudge their curiosity about her tragic circumstances; it was human nature to be fascinated with the pain of others. Maddie understood it was part concern and part fear. After all, she was the living embodiment of a life turned horribly wrong in the blink of an eye, and it must be hard for those around her not to worry the same level of unimaginable horror could befall them.

With a quiet sigh, she listened as the two women bantered about the effects of holiday bingeing on their waistlines while they prepared their lunches, and she let her own thoughts of the holidays come to the forefront of her mind.

The thought of the Christmas season had filled her with dread since the moment it had first crossed her thoughts after the accident.

Contemplating any semblance of celebration in an empty house haunted by the echoes of laughter and love had seemed abhorrent to her.

Maddie's mother, Claire, had suggested they take a trip abroad to escape, but Christmas is a global phenomenon, and a change of scenery would do nothing to fill the void left by death.

At the thought of her headstrong and resilient mother, Maddie silently thanked the heavens yet again for giving her such a solid rock to lean on. She couldn't have survived the last eight months without Claire.

Claire had always taught Maddie to focus on the needs of others to keep from being too absorbed with yourself, and although Maddie had seen her mother live that philosophy her entire life, it had never been more evident than when Claire had cast aside her own grief and loss to help Maddie survive in the difficult months following the accident.

Following Claire's example had inspired Maddie to return to work, where she could put the needs of her students ahead of her own and allow her work to consume her.

The road was long and hard, and there were many times when Maddie had been certain it would be easier if she could give up and join her beloved husband and daughter in the ground. But day by day, minute by minute, she'd continued moving forward.

Maddie knew she had to get on with her life, but she was determined to do something with it that would make Simon and Corrine proud. Something that would in any way justify her being alive with them both dead.

It wasn't enough to merely survive and force herself to get out of bed every day. She needed a reason to live, a purpose. Her students gave her that.

She glanced in the restroom's lone mirror and tilted her head to one side, surveying her reflection.

The color was slowly returning to her cheeks, though they were still sunken from the weight she'd lost. The dark circles under her eyes had diminished slightly since she'd decided what to do about Christmas and finally found some measure of peace.

The decision hadn't been easy to make, but Maddie was

certain it was the right one, and she reassured herself with a slight nod. No one at school knew about her plans yet, a deliberate choice to delay the inevitable questions and judgements.

But in the long run, what did it matter what they thought?

They had their own lives and their own families to concern them.

Why should her house be empty and hauntingly silent for Christmas when she could fill it with love and laughter again?

She wasn't the only one hurting and in need of a family to call her own.

It had started with a student named Stevie. More than any other, this young girl had pulled at Maddie's heartstrings. Maddie had sensed something wasn't right at home, but it took a while to earn Stevie's trust enough for the girl to confide the truth—her mother had abandoned her, and she'd been living alone.

Maddie couldn't conceive how any mother could leave her child that way, especially when Maddie would have given anything to hold Corinne once again.

She acted quickly to get Stevie help, but the system hadn't proven much of a rescue. Stevie had been bounced around a number of group homes, and Maddie felt helpless as the light faded from the young girl's eyes and her bright, talkative personality became more sullen and withdrawn.

Stevie's fate began to consume Maddie's thoughts, and the more she deliberated, the more certain she was that she had to do something. Stevie was a daughter in need of mothering, and Maddie was a mother whose empty arms ached. In addition to that painful connection, the two of them were genuinely fond of each other, and they'd formed a strong bond, the likes of which Maddie had never had with a student.

Of course, when the idea of adopting Stevie had first come

to her, Maddie had dismissed it as disloyal to Corinne's memory.

"Nonsense!" Claire had exclaimed when Maddie finally confided her thoughts one evening over dinner. "You living a life alone and devoid of love won't bring our sweet girl back, and I know that's not what Corinne or Simon would want for you."

Maddie had held her breath as she blinked back tears.

"So, you think it's a good idea, then? You think I should adopt Stevie?"

Claire had sat back in her chair and folded her napkin to lay it on the table.

"I suppose there are some who will say it's too soon. They'll say you may be making impulsive decisions based in grief, and that you may not be in your right mind to make choices with such long-lasting effects on both you and this young girl."

Claire paused, and Maddie leaned forward, anxious to hear her mother's opinion.

"But what do *you* say, Mom?"

"I know you well enough to know you wouldn't seriously consider this if you hadn't thought it through, and you wouldn't be telling me if you hadn't already come to the conclusion that it's a good idea."

It wasn't enough. Maddie needed to know she would have Claire's support. She couldn't pursue such a large undertaking without it.

"But you agree that it's a good idea, right?"

Claire's gaze was steady as she looked at her daughter and took the time to choose her words with care.

"Love is rarely a bad idea, Madeline. But let's not sugar-coat or minimize the weight of this decision. You're still a young woman, you know. At thirty-four, you have many years ahead of you, God willing, and I pray you've already been dealt all the tragedy you'll face. I don't need to tell you what a big commitment this is, what a big step it will be for both of you. You are promising this girl you will be there for her from this point forth, come what may. You are taking on the responsibility, emotionally and financially, for someone else's child."

"I know," Maddie said. "I understand. But I have the means to support her financially. I have the training and the background to help her emotionally. And I realize people will think I'm doing this to somehow replace—" Her voice fell away, and she couldn't bring herself to say her daughter's name attached to such a thought.

Claire's eyes filled with tears as she reached across the table to take Maddie's hand.

"No one will ever replace Corinne. No one ever could. Nor will anyone ever fill her space in your heart. But the heart has many chambers, and its capacity for love knows no bounds."

Memories of Corinne flashed through Maddie's mind, and she closed her eyes against the pain they brought. Nothing would bring her daughter back. She couldn't be the mother she'd wanted to be for Corinne. That had been ripped away in one single devastating moment. But she could be a mother again. She could make someone else's life better.

She opened her eyes and gave Claire's hand a squeeze.

"I want to give Stevie a home. I want to give her love and stability, like you've given me. I want to encourage her and support her and help her achieve her dreams. I want her to wake up every day knowing someone believes in her and is there for her."

"You want to be a mother again."

The tears streamed down Maddie's cheeks as she nodded. "Yes. Yes, I do."

"Then bring her home, and we'll love her like she was our own."

Maddie knew she'd need to get the ball rolling quickly if she hoped to bring Stevie home before Christmas. She didn't know what might be involved in the approval process, but luckily, she had contacts within the system who could answer her questions and help her navigate the mounds of paperwork and red tape.

She learned that despite the fact that Stevie's mother had vanished, the parental rights had not been legally terminated, so Maddie couldn't move to adopt Stevie outright. Instead, she'd have to foster toward adoption, knowing that could only take place if something happened to terminate the mother's rights.

The adoption agency was very upfront with Maddie in conveying that the ultimate goal was for Stevie to be reunited with a healthier version of her mother if she turned back up. Maddie found it hard to hope for that outcome. She couldn't imagine that a parent who had willingly abandoned her child and left her to fend on her own would return a changed woman, but she'd take Stevie however she could get her and hope for the best for them both.

"I don't suppose you'd have room for two?" asked Natalie, the agency worker assigned to Maddie, as they talked one day.

"Oh, no, I don't think so," Maddie answered, but as Natalie began to describe Alissa, a ten-year-old who had lost both parents in a car accident, Maddie quickly reconsidered.

The girl was the same age Corinne had been when she died, and Alissa's parents had both worked at the university with Maddie's late husband, Simon. She and Alissa had both been robbed of their family without warning and thrust into a new life completely foreign to the one they'd known before.

How could she say no? She had plenty of room in the big old house, and as someone who'd always wanted a sister when she was growing up, Maddie thought perhaps Alissa and Stevie would be good for each other.

Because Alissa had no known family with ties to her, Maddie would be able to adopt her after a period of fostering.

Eager to make the transition as smooth as possible for the girls, she arranged for them both to arrive on the day after school let out for the Christmas break. That would give Maddie two weeks with them, time to adjust and bond before they all went back to the daily routine of school and work.

For the first time since the accident, hope blossomed in Maddie's heart. She smiled more readily, and she even laughed a few times without feeling guilty. She'd gone from dreading the upcoming holidays to readying the house for the girls' arrival.

Her newfound joy even gave her the courage to face a task she'd known was necessary but hadn't yet been able to face—going into Corinne's room to pack her things.

"Are you sure you want to do this?" Claire asked as they stood outside the bedroom door. "We could easily convert that room by Simon's study into a nice bedroom for Alissa, and you could have Stevie downstairs in the room off the kitchen like you'd planned."

Maddie shook her head as her hand wavered above the knob. "No. I don't want Alissa up here alone. I want her and Stevie on the same floor together, so they have each other. I have to do this eventually, and I want it done before the girls get here. It's not healthy to keep everything preserved in here like it's some sort of tomb or mausoleum in the house."

She threw the door open and took in a deep breath against the assault of emotions that hit her every time she entered her daughter's room.

"I know it's the right decision, but God, it hurts," she whispered. "It's like saying goodbye all over again and facing the fact that my baby girl isn't coming home. It makes it seem even more final."

Claire swallowed against the lump in her throat as she nodded. "We have to remember these are only physical reminders. Corinne lives in our hearts and in our memories, not in these material things."

At first, the two women worked in silence as they folded Corinne's clothes and stacked them into boxes. The memories were a constant barrage, and a random shirt or jacket could easily bring forth quiet sobs, but as they moved through the books, toys, and mementos from Corinne's short life, they found moments of laughter as well, and a bittersweet release in letting go.

"This house will be filled with love," Claire said when they'd finished the project that had seemed insurmountable before it began. "This room will provide a sanctuary to a young soul who desperately needs it, and I like to think that would make our Corinne very happy."

Maddie had expected to feel empowered by finishing Corinne's room, but as she considered decorating the house for Christmas, she discovered that it was much too difficult to think about using the items she and Simon had gathered and shared over the course of their marriage and Corinne's childhood. Just the thought of going into the attic to pull it all down was daunting, and the idea of seeing those reminders every day of the holiday season was too much to bear.

"I've decided to get new decorations for the house," Maddie announced to Claire over dinner one night. "Everything I have now is tied to Simon and Corinne. I will always have my memories of past Christmases, and I know Alissa and Stevie will have their own memories, too. But if the three of us are going to make a fresh start, there needs to be a clean slate. New decorations. New traditions. New memories."

Claire didn't answer.

"Mom, are you listening to me?"

"Yes, dear," Claire replied without so much as even a glance in Maddie's direction.

"Okay, so I guess you'd be totally okay with my renting live reindeer to prance around my living room on Christmas morning. I mean, we can shovel the poop into the fireplace for fuel, right?"

"Yes, dear."

"Mom!" Maddie shrieked. "You haven't heard a word I've said. I just told you I'm going to shovel reindeer poop in my living room, and you were fine with it. What's up with you? You've been preoccupied since I got here, giving me one-word answers and an occasional nod here and there. What's going on?"

Claire pressed her lips together in a frown. "I don't think I should mention it."

"Mention what? What's wrong?"

Maddie leaned forward to rest her hand on her mother's arm, and Claire put her hand over Maddie's and squeezed.

"Nothing's *wrong*. Oh, Madeline. Do you remember Maeve, the sweet lady who was the town librarian for years upon years? I had lunch with Marjorie today. She's working at the high school now as the office secretary. Well, she told me sad news about Maeve's granddaughter, Josephine. Marjorie says she's a real sweet girl. A good student and a hard worker. But she's had the roughest luck. As you know, both of her parents died when she was younger, so Maeve was raising her. I assumed when Maeve passed away that someone else in the family had taken the girl in. But it turns out there was no one in the family to claim her. She was placed in foster care, and Marjorie says Josephine's in a terrible situation. She's certain they're using the poor girl as free labor, and she suspects they might be abusive."

"That's horrible."

Maddie's heart hurt just thinking about it. She knew Maeve would have been devastated for her granddaughter to be all alone, so young, and with no family to turn to. How terrified Josephine must have been when her grandmother died!

It wasn't like Maddie hadn't always known these struggles existed, but it seemed that since she'd decided to intervene on Stevie's behalf, she'd been confronted with the reality of other young girls on their own who were equally deserving of love and stability and a place to truly call home.

Claire sighed. "I know you've got your hands full with the two already coming, but I wish we could do something to help Maeve's granddaughter. Marjorie said she's so bright, and she'd have a wonderful future ahead of her if she could just catch a break."

Maddie set down her fork as her eyes widened. "Are you saying you want me to adopt a third?"

"Well, you do have that room downstairs. You'd originally thought to put Stevie in there to be close to you. What if you did that and gave Josephine the room next to Simon's study?"

"I think my plate is going to be rather full with suddenly having two kids who might have God only knows what kind of issues from their circumstances. I don't know that I could do another."

"I understand what you're saying, and I knew it was a long shot. That's why I hesitated to mention it. It's just that with her being fifteen, her chances of getting adopted aren't that great. People don't often want the older teens. I swear I'd take her myself if I thought the state would approve me, but my retirement community is no place for a teenager, and I'm old and set in my ways. Oh, well. I guess we can't save them all."

Claire changed the subject and they didn't touch on it again that night, but Josephine never strayed far from Maddie's thoughts over the next few days. She remembered often seeing the young girl at the library before Maeve died. Maddie wasn't sure how old Josephine had been when her parents died but knew she had been quite young. She wondered how long the girl had been in foster care. Had Maeve been gone already last Christmas? Or was this Josephine's first Christmas with no family?

If Josephine was in a bad foster situation—bad enough that the school secretary was aware of it—then surely the social workers assigned to her could step in and place her somewhere better.

But what if there was no place better available?

Claire was right—Maddie couldn't save every child trapped in the system, and she kept telling herself she was doing her part by taking in two children already. But no matter what logic she tried to apply, her mind kept returning to Josephine's plight, and by the end of the week, she knew she had to at least try and improve Josephine's situation.

She called Natalie to inquire about the girl, and Natalie called back the next day saying there was little that could be done since Josephine had already been placed with a family.

"But what if I was to adopt her?" Maddie asked.

"In addition to Stevie and Alissa? You sure you want to do that?"

"Just look into it for me. Let me know if it's possible. See if I can get approved for all three girls."

Natalie's reply a few days later was that yes, Maddie could move forward with adopting Josephine if she chose to, but it would take a miracle to get things rolling in time for Christmas. Josephine likely wouldn't be able to join them until after the first of the new year.

Though disappointed, Maddie resigned herself to the fact, but it didn't stop her from shopping for the girl while she was out and about picking up things for the other two.

She and Claire had decided they wouldn't buy too many clothes and personal items for the girls, preferring to take them and let them pick out things according to their own tastes once they'd arrived.

Knowing they'd each probably want to choose their own

bedroom decor, she stuck to basic neutrals when outfitting the three rooms, hoping to create a warm and welcoming environment for them to come into. It would be easy enough to let them personalize their own space once they got settled.

By the time the last week of school rolled around before the Christmas break, the house was decked out with wreaths, ribbons, and lights inside and out. She'd picked one special gift for Stevie and Alissa to receive when they arrived, and a few other items were wrapped and waiting under the tree.

The week seemed to be dragging on forever, and Maddie was counting down the hours until she'd be able to finally have the girls under her roof where they could start their new lives together.

It was early morning Thursday when she got a call that Josephine had been injured in the home where she was being fostered. Though the injury was minor and would allow a full recovery, the circumstances surrounding it had triggered an investigation that found the foster parents to be unfit. All the fostered children were to be removed from the home, and Josephine needed a placement right away.

Maddie gladly accepted, and she rushed around after school to get last-minute items for Josephine's bedroom and gifts to put under the tree in preparation for her arrival the next day.

As she sat at the kitchen table that night sipping a cup of bedtime tea, Maddie's mind spun with the reality that she would soon have three girls in her care, all of whom would need particular attention and loads of love to heal what had transpired in their pasts.

She stood and walked through her house, room by room, allowing memories of Simon and Corinne to wash over her. She'd give anything to have them back, to turn back time and prevent the horrific accident that had taken them from her.

If only she hadn't locked her keys in the car after staying late at school that night. If only the custodian or someone on the security force had been there to help her. She wouldn't have needed to call Simon to come and get her. He and Corrine wouldn't have been on the road. They'd still be here with her, excited for Christmas morning.

Maddie stopped in front of the tree, the myriad of colored lights blurring through her tears.

She knew that it did no good to go over the what ifs again. She'd been through them countless times since that night.

What had been done could not be undone. What had been lost could not be given back.

Her only option was to move forward. To live a life that was full of love. To try and be worthy of Simon and Corinne's memories in all she said and did.

The shrill ringing of the phone startled her, and she sloshed tea on her hand.

She was surprised to hear Natalie's voice on the other end. It was well past office hours, though she'd learned that social workers rarely stick to a set schedule.

"I'm so sorry to call so late, Maddie, but time is of the essence, and you were the first person I thought of."

"What's wrong?" Maddie asked, wary of what might have happened to cause Natalie such distress. "Is it the girls? Has something happened to one of the girls?"

"No. They're fine. Josephine will be coming to you tomorrow, and Alissa and Stevie will arrive on Saturday. I just got a call from a foster family to inform me that they are going out of town for the holidays and will not be taking their foster child."

"How can they do that? Are they allowed to do that?"

"They're allowed to take a trip without her, but they're supposed to give me enough notice to find a suitable temporary placement for the poor girl. Now, I've got to go get her a couple of days before Christmas and take her to a new place with people she's never met for her to spend the holiday. She's only eight years old, and—"

"Say no more," Maddie said, her heart offering before her mind even had time to consider. "We've got plenty of room. Bring her here."

"Are you sure? I know you've got three coming, but I thought since they're all starting out together in a new place, it may be less awkward for this little one, Hailey. It would be a temporary placement, but if you could—"

"Natalie, you know as well as I do that once she gets here, she won't need to leave. Don't worry about that. She has a long-term placement right here. Now, I've already taken the day off tomorrow to welcome Josephine and do a few last-minute preparations for her and the other girls. If you can give me Hailey's sizes and her interests, I'll run out tomorrow and get a few things to put under the tree for her. She'll need to share a room with Alissa since they're closest in age, so hopefully that will work out well."

After writing down the details Natalie could give her on Hailey, Maddie hung up the phone and sat back down at the table to sip her tea.

Four girls. Four opportunities to show love.

She was going from a bereaved widow who'd lost her only child to mothering four daughters.

She smiled at the thought of what Simon might say, and she pictured Corinne's sweet grin.

Perhaps there were a couple of traditions she'd carry over into her new life—like Simon's insistence on having blueberry waffles on Christmas morning and Corinne's letters to Santa.

The memories filled her with joy, and the idea of what the future would bring filled her with hope. She went to bed with a heart at peace, ready to welcome her new family but steadfast in the knowledge that nothing could replace or diminish the family she'd had.

❄

JO O'MALLEY

AUTHOR TAMMY L. GRACE

Mrs. Ashburn plucked the glasses from the beaded chain around her neck, where they rested against her drab blouse, and perched them on the end of her nose. Her eyes scanned the note in her hand and then flicked over the top of her glasses. "Miss O'Malley," she hollered. "You're to take your things and report to the office."

Her not so subtle announcement elicited snickers and giggles from the class. Jo didn't bother saying goodbye to any of her classmates before trudging down the hallway to her locker and stuffing the library books she had picked up at lunch into her worn backpack. She grabbed the one strap still attached to the top, and let the frayed one drag along the tile floor.

Laughter and merriment spilled from the classrooms into the hallway as classes held their holiday celebrations. Despite the buzz of excitement around Jo, worry and angst filled her thoughts.

The bag was heavy and she took her time getting to the office at Granite Ridge High. Marjorie, the secretary who had known her grandmother smiled at Jo, but it was a pity smile. Jo's heart pounded in her chest. What could she have done to warrant a summons to the office? It couldn't be an overdue meal bill since as humiliating as it was, she was on free lunch now.

Marjorie's eyes darted to the far corner of the office. Mrs. Wacker, her social worker stood there. Her weary eyes gave Jo the same uninspired look she always displayed. "Josephine," she said.

Jo rolled her eyes. *Why can she never remember to call me Jo?* As Jo grumbled, she noticed her tattered cloth bag from Mountain Drugs & Books in Mrs. Wacker's fleshy hand. She had that huggable body shape that made you think of a sweet grandma who loved to bake and cuddle, but she'd never offered Jo so much as an ounce of kindness.

"I had Marjorie send someone to collect your gym clothes." The social worker, bundled in a heavy coat, dipped her head in Marjorie's direction and ushered Jo into the main hallway toward the entrance. "I've got some unexpected news."

Dread crept up Jo's neck. She shoved the door open and a blast of cold air sucked away what little breath she had left.

Mrs. Wacker toddled across the sidewalk, breathing heavily. "I know you haven't been happy at the Monroe's ranch."

That was the understatement of the year. Mr. and Mrs. Monroe were leeches who made it clear they took in foster kids for the money and for what Jo thought of as slave labor at their ranch. Jo had been telling Wacker the Slacker and anyone else who would listen about their fraudulent activities for the last year.

Mrs. Wacker pointed at her dingy gray sedan with government plates. She unlocked it and reached into the backseat. "I picked up your things from the ranch," she said, holding the trash bag up like a trophy.

Jo's head swiveled around the parking lot, looking to see if anyone was watching her and the depressing bag that represented her meager belongings. "Could you please put it in the car before anyone sees?" Jo shook her head with disgust and flung her backpack next to the trash bag, before getting into the passenger seat.

Mrs. Wacker situated her bulk behind the wheel and let out a long sigh. "For reasons I cannot discuss, Mr. and Mrs. Monroe are no longer certified foster parents."

Jo fingered the bandage on her hand and suppressed a smile. The injury from the hay hook had required treatment at urgent care, which had meant a report of the incident to Mrs. Wacker. Jo also made sure her guidance counselor at the high school saw it and knew what had happened. Jo knew full well what could not be discussed. She had lived it for the last year.

"I'm driving you to your new home where you'll meet your new foster mother, Mrs. Kirby."

The momentary elation was fleeting. Jo swallowed a lump in her throat. "What about Nathan and Molly? Where are they going?" Jo's throat burned and her mouth went dry, as if she hasn't tasted water in days. "I can't leave them there. I won't."

Mrs. Wacker's frosted pink lips curved between her pudgy cheeks. "Don't get upset, Josephine." She reached to pat Jo's arm.

"It's Jo," she said, through gritted teeth. "I've told you that for a year and you never remember."

Mrs. Wacker tsked. "I can't possibly remember everyone's nickname now, can I?" She steered the car from the school and added, "You really need to control your temper, my dear. Nathan and Molly's aunt agreed to take them. They're on their way to Boise to get a flight to Kentucky. Placing kids with someone in the family is really the ideal situation." Mrs. Wacker beamed with delight, as if she had been the one to orchestrate such a success.

"Unless, of course, you don't have any family," Jo mumbled. She turned and looked out the window, letting her breath fog it as she took in the festive decorations along Main

Street and the smiling townsfolk milling about the sidewalks, toting holiday shopping bags.

"I didn't even get to say goodbye to them," she whispered. But that was nothing new. They were just the latest in a string of people in her life who had disappeared without a word.

The brakes on Mrs. Wacker's sedan squealed as she parked in front of a huge brick Victorian home. Colorful lights graced the intricate roofline and wrapped around the columns on the porch. The resemblance to one of those fancy gingerbread houses Jo had seen on television wasn't lost on her. The door held a huge fresh wreath and the glow of warm lights filled every window, even the ones in the turret that rose above the highest roof peak.

Her cheeks flushed with embarrassment as she lugged the trash bag and her ratty backpack up the steps. Mrs. Wacker ambled after her, clutching the bag of dirty gym clothes to her chest. When she made it to the porch, she used her gloved finger to poke the doorbell. A soft series of chimes drifted from inside the house.

The door opened and a woman with gentle brown eyes and a warm smile greeted them, along with the mouth-watering aroma of freshly baked sugar cookies, bringing Grandma Maeve immediately to mind. But that's where the similarity ended. The woman was tall, and wore stylish heeled boots, jeans, and a teal green poncho with a shimmery fringe over a matching turtleneck. Jo studied her face, thinking she recognized her, barely listening as Mrs. Wacker droned on making introductions.

Mrs. Kirby extended her hand, revealing a sparkly silver and teal beaded bracelet, and offered to take Jo's backpack. "Let me help you with your things, Jo?"

When Jo heard her voice, she realized why Mrs. Kirby seemed familiar. She was a school counselor at Jo's old school. Jo remembered her as friendly and nice, although she never had much interaction with her. She smiled back at Mrs. Kirby and said, "Yes, and thank you."

Mrs. Wacker stuffed the cloth bag in Jo's arms, promised she'd be in touch after the first of the year, and scurried down the steps. Jo ignored her, focusing instead on the breathtaking entryway and huge staircase, draped with greenery.

Mrs. Kirby led Jo up the staircase. "I don't know if Mrs. Wacker told you, but I've decided to open my home to four children, all girls. You're the oldest, so I wanted you to have this room up here adjacent to the turret, so you'll have some privacy."

She waved her hand around the space outfitted with built in bookshelves filled with leather bound books, a huge desk, and oversized chairs. "This was Mr. Kirby's office, so it's a bit masculine, but I love the dark colors and it gets plenty of light from all the windows." Jo detected sadness in her voice when she mentioned her husband and realized despite her friendly smile, there was a hint of sorrow in Mrs. Kirby's eyes.

Jo looked around the space again. She didn't care what color the furnishings were and imagined herself lounging in the comfortable chair, reading a book by the fire. She followed Mrs. Kirby to the bedroom and gazed at the room decorated in shades of pale and dark green. A thick area rug covered part of the hardwood floor and she took care not to walk on it. The room resembled those she imagined when reading her beloved novels of Jane Austen and Emily Bronte.

She dropped the trash bag on the floor. "My clean clothes have been jumbled with my dirty ones. Do you have a washing machine I could use?"

"Of course, I'll show you the laundry room and how to work the machines. In the meantime, I got you an early

Christmas gift." She removed a package with shimmering ribbons from the dresser and handed it to Jo.

Tears stung Jo's eyes as she read the glittery card attached to the box. *Merry Christmas, Jo. I hope this is the first of many we will spend together. With love, Mrs. Kirby.*

Maybe this was more than a temporary placement. Jo's heart raced at the thought of being able to live in a home like this one with someone who seemed to truly care about her. Someone with a kind heart and room for four foster girls.

She opened the box, taking care to save the gorgeous ribbon, and unearthed a pair of shearling lined boots. She hadn't had new shoes or clothes since before Grandma Maeve had passed away, and let her fingers run over the soft boots.

The hand-me-downs she wore each day to school were becoming more and more threadbare, and her tennis shoes were almost completely worn. "If you don't like them or they don't fit, we can take them back and get something else. I thought we'd go shopping once the other girls arrive and you can all pick out some new jeans and sweaters or whatever else you need." Mrs. Kirby smiled, but looked uneasy, as if she wasn't sure Jo liked the boots.

"They're beautiful. I love them. I, uh, just didn't expect them," Jo said, wiping a finger under her eye.

Mrs. Kirby's smile deepened. "Oh, good, I wasn't sure. Like I said, they're easy to exchange if they don't fit." She showed Jo where things were located and gave her a quick tour of the space. "I'll give you some time to get settled and then just come downstairs. I've got dinner about ready and then you can do your laundry, read, watch television, whatever you'd like. If you're tired, you can make it an early night."

Jo noticed a selection of skin care products and the ointment and bandages on the counter in the bathroom, amazed that Mrs. Kirby had thought of everything she needed. She hurried back to the bedroom and tried on the boots, finding fluffy socks wedged into each toe. She pulled off the ones she wore, with holes in each heel. The boots were warm and so comfortable.

Despite wanting to toss her old shoes and socks, she added them to the trash bag, not convinced this home would last long and not wanting to throw away anything she might need later. Holey socks and too short pants were better than none.

The bed, with a fluffy comforter the color of cream and a beautiful velvety throw in forest green, beckoned her to try it and she rested her head against the pillows, letting her body relax for the first time since she had been placed in care. She shut her eyes, hoping this wasn't just a Christmas placement, knowing full well how some people felt guilty during the holidays and wanted to treat foster kids to something special. She wanted to believe what Mrs. Kirby had written in her card was genuine.

The next day, Jo slept in and then lost herself in Mr. Kirby's bookshelves, running her fingers across the soft, leather-bound volumes. The comfortable space, where the almost musty aroma of the older books mingled with the rich scent of the leather furniture, was Jo's idea of heaven. She lingered there until the sound of the doorbell chimes interrupted her musings and she hustled from the study and down the stairs.

When she arrived, Mrs. Kirby was ushering in three girls, all of them wide-eyed. Jo's heart broke when she saw the youngest one, Hailey, a tiny girl with glasses, no more than second grade, like Molly had been. At least Jo hadn't had to go into foster care until she was older. She couldn't imagine spending her entire childhood like she had spent the last year.

Next, Mrs. Kirby introduced Stevie, who towered over the two younger girls. Freckles dotted her face, framed by fiery red hair, and there was a harshness in her stance and wariness in her eyes that signaled the thirteen-year-old didn't trust easily.

The sweet and petite girl next to her was ten-year-old Alissa. Her big brown eyes were the size of saucers. The two youngest held their trash bags close to them, clinging to what was familiar, uncertainty conveyed in tiny creases in their foreheads.

Mrs. Kirby was gentle with them and took each of the younger girls by the hand, talking in a soft and reassuring voice. After the initial greetings, Jo followed everyone upstairs, carrying Alissa's and Hailey's bags. While the girls explored their rooms and situated their belongings, rather than stand around and gawk at them, Jo sunk into the chair in the study, and picked up the book she had been reading. After everyone had settled into their rooms and gotten acquainted with the layout, Mrs. Kirby suggested they head downstairs to dinner.

Mrs. Kirby led them through the foyer, past the formal dining room and the family room where a huge tree stood next to a window, and into the large kitchen. Last night, Jo had been in a fog, overwhelmed by all the changes, the idea of staying with Mrs. Kirby, and imagining what the three girls might be like, and hadn't taken the time to notice much beyond her bedroom and the study.

Now, past the shock of it all, she surveyed the space in more detail. Everywhere Jo looked, there were beautiful Christmas decorations, twinkling lights, and the whole house smelled of fresh pine. In the corner, a casual wooden table with built in bench seating, decorated with holiday pillows, was set for dinner. Jo had never seen a more beautiful home and hoped again that this wasn't just a temporary placement.

Mrs. Kirby directed the girls to a sink in the mud room where they could wash their hands before taking a seat at the table. Stevie stood in front of the huge granite counter and offered to help Mrs. Kirby with preparations. Jo took charge of the younger girls and got them situated at the table, pouring milk into their glasses, and pointing out some of the beautiful decorations and ornaments tucked in every corner.

Jo marveled at the matching plates and silverware and the fresh flowers in the center of the table. The roast chicken and vegetables were flavorful and delicious. At Mrs. Kirby's urging, she stuffed herself with a second helping of mashed potatoes and gravy. After the meal, Mrs. Kirby said she'd like each of the girls to write a letter to Santa.

Jo offered to help with the dishes, but Mrs. Kirby told her to relax instead and that there would be plenty of time to figure out household chores and responsibilities, but for tonight she only needed to write her letter. Mrs. Kirby bent closer to Jo and whispered, "I know you may not believe in Santa, but help me keep the magic alive for Alissa and Hailey."

Jo took a piece of paper and a pencil and wandered into the family room, next to the tree. As she listened to the soft Christmas music coming from the speakers, she contemplated what to write. She hadn't believed in Santa for several years, but despite her disbelief, her grandma had always made sure she received a special gift from the jolly elf. She felt the tightness in her throat and the sting of tears. This time of year was tough without Grandma Maeve.

Dear Santa, I feel more than silly doing this, since I know you're not real and I'm too old to believe in you, but I can tell writing down my Christmas wish is important to Mrs. Kirby. More than anything, I'd like this feeling I have right now, the one where I am safe and it feels like this could be home and I'm not alone, but have a real family and sisters, to last forever.

In the days that followed, leading up to Christmas, Jo began to feel more at ease. As they shared meals and visited, the girls relaxed more, and the anxious eyes Jo had faced when the other three girls had arrived, had been replaced by smiles and even some giggles from the two youngest.

Mrs. Kirby suggested a trip to town so they could all do a bit of secret Christmas shopping for each other. They strolled through the stores and as they walked, Mrs. Kirby chatted with them about things they liked and pointed out items on the shelves to see what sparked an interest in each of the girls. After they wandered together a bit, Mrs. Kirby gave Jo and Stevie the freedom to duck into the shops along Main Street, giving each of them some money so they could pick out gifts for the others.

When Jo walked into Mountain Drugs and Books, she shut her eyes and thought back to all the times she and Grandma Maeve had spent in the store. If she didn't think too hard, and let the scents from the perfumes and lotions, from the sugared candies lined up along the counter in big glass jars, permeate her senses, she could almost believe it was years ago. Those familiar scents and the underlying essence of new books comforted her. She had missed spending time downtown, going to Rusty's Café for pie, and lingering at the library or plopping into a chair here in the bookstore and reading all afternoon.

She hadn't been able to do any of those things, much less spend time in town, after being taken in by the Monroe family. She relished the bit of freedom afforded her and lingered over the choices, lost in happier memories as she selected gifts for the girls she had just met, hoping this might not be a dream and they might all be together long after Christmas.

Mrs. Kirby loaded the shopping bags in her car, making sure to keep the bags separate, so there was no chance of peeking. As dusk began to settle over Granite Ridge, she drove them home. Jo couldn't help but smile when Alissa and Hailey gasped, their eyes filled with wonder, when they glimpsed the huge house illuminated with what had to be thousands of festive lights.

Alissa and Hailey pointed at different spots in the yard, calling out their favorite colors and gawking at the rows of lights along the roofline. Their eyes reflected not only the sparkle of the lights, but the true wonder of the season. Jo helped carry the shopping bags and stood at the end of the driveway, captivated by the twinkling display and the warmth that radiated from the glow of soft lights, matched only by the heart of Mrs. Kirby, who smiled as she watched the girls and brushed a finger under her eyes.

Christmas morning, Jo, wearing the new red flannel nightgown she had found under her pillow last night, tiptoed past the closed door of the bedroom shared by Alissa and Hailey, and made her way downstairs. Mrs. Kirby and Stevie were in the kitchen, both donning Christmas aprons over their red flannel nightgowns as they worked at the large granite counter.

"Merry Christmas, Jo," said Mrs. Kirby. "We're just getting breakfast together, so we can have a bite to eat after we open presents."

Listening to Stevie over dinner the last couple of nights, Jo had learned she enjoyed cooking. From the smile on her face as she helped Mrs. Kirby put the finishing touches on a braided pastry, it was evident she was happiest when she was creating something in the kitchen.

The decadent pastry, covered in slivered almonds and powdered sugar, looked delicious, as did the cheesy egg casserole Mrs. Kirby was making. She explained that Mr. Kirby had a tradition of having blueberry waffles on

Christmas morning and hoped the girls would enjoy them. Stevie beamed when she was put in charge of making them.

Soon, they heard Hailey and Alissa scurrying down the stairs. Jo peeked around the corner and spied Hailey, carrying her little stuffed dog, Charlie, and holding hands with Alissa as they both stared at the tree. Both of them fidgeted with excitement to open presents, and couldn't resist touching a few of the shiny packages. Jo hated to admit it, but even she was excited to open presents. Last Christmas, the first without Grandma Maeve, had been miserable, but these last few days with Mrs. Kirby gave her a glimmer of hope.

Jo couldn't help but smile and felt Mrs. Kirby's hand on her shoulder as she joined in watching them. Instead of worrying about breakfast, Mrs. Kirby popped the casserole and the pastry into the oven to bake and suggested they open gifts and then enjoy their meal. While Jo took charge of keeping an eye on the two youngest, Stevie made hot chocolate for everyone. Mrs. Kirby added her own mug of hot tea to the tray she carried into the family room, where the girls sat cross-legged in front of the tree, anxiously waiting, while they eyed the tags on the mountain of gifts under the tree.

Mrs. Kirby passed out the gifts and asked all the girls to watch as each one opened their boxes. Shrieks of delight came from Alissa and Hailey as they opened their puzzles, books, pens, and pencils. Like the other girls, Jo had taken the money Mrs. Kirby had given her and tried to find meaningful gifts, keeping in mind Hailey's affection for dogs, Stevie's ambitions in the kitchen, and Alissa's love of books. Choosing Mrs. Kirby's gift was harder, but Jo settled on a rhinestone encrusted picture frame and included a note that it was meant to hold a photo of all of them celebrating their first Christmas together.

Jo treasured the hair ribbon from Hailey, the journal from Alissa, and the fancy gourmet fudge from Stevie, along with the sturdy new backpack from Mrs. Kirby. More than the gifts, she cherished the tender smiles from each of them. These three girls had found a way into her heart, and along with the kind woman who had opened her home to all of them, they already felt like family.

When Mrs. Kirby opened Jo's gift, tears dotted her cheeks. She gathered the girls closer to her, scrunching them together by stretching her arms around them, and used her phone to capture the moment. She gazed at the photo and said, "This is so very special and is the true meaning of Christmas. I'm so thankful you're all here to spend it with me." She clutched the frame to her chest. "You don't know how much this means to me. We'll have to take our picture every year, just like this one."

From the little things Mrs. Kirby mentioned and the way she spoke about their future, Jo sensed that Mrs. Kirby needed the four girls as much as they needed her.

After they finished the yummy breakfast, Jo and Stevie did the dishes and cleaned up the kitchen, while Mrs. Kirby got the younger girls organized and ready to meet Mrs. Kirby's mother, Claire, who was due to arrive later in the morning.

After, Jo went upstairs to her room and dressed in a new sweater, a deep copper color that brought out the highlights in her brown hair, then she took her new journal to the oversized chair near the bookcase in Mr. Kirby's office. She had already placed her beloved copy of *To Kill A Mockingbird* that Grandma Maeve had given her on one of the shelves, and now was anxious to read the leather volume resting next to it.

Mrs. Kirby shared that her husband had been a professor in the philosophy department and had amassed a huge collection of books, and that Jo was welcome to read any of them. Jo had chosen *Middlemarch*, fascinated by the idea of a woman writing under a man's name, and was eyeing the Shakespeare collection for her next read. She slouched across the chair, letting her legs dangle over the arm. Quickly, she admired her new boots, then checked the time. Mrs. Kirby's mother, who hoped the girls would call her Nan, was due to arrive in a few minutes. Jo wrote the date at the top of the first page of her journal before jotting an entry.

I think my letter to Santa worked. This last year has eaten away at me. I wasn't convinced I could trust Mrs. Kirby, but she's given me new hope. Her genuine kindness and love shine through in all that she does for us. She's patient and warm, but isn't going to put up with any shenanigans, as Grandma Maeve would say. She wants us to be a family, soul sisters, she says. She explained although we aren't related by blood, the term means we're kindred spirits and we'll always be linked by a bond that transcends time and distance. I like the idea that no matter what happens, we'll always have each other. I've felt lonely for so long, except for Grandma Maeve, and losing her made me realize just how harsh the world can be. I didn't think anyone cared and that no one ever would again. But now I have sisters. Sisters of my heart. I have a family! Please, please, please, make it be real.

STEVIE FOX

AUTHOR EV BISHOP

Her jaw was clenched so tightly that her teeth ached, but Stevie thought that was probably preferable to standing there with her hands balled into fists, looking like she wanted to punch somebody.

Her latest social worker, Natalie, a hideously cheerful woman who always insisted that whatever new family she stuck Stevie into could be "the one," pressed the ornate, old-fashioned doorbell. A series of musical chimes rang somewhere deep inside the house. While they waited for Mrs. Kirby to answer the door—still so weird that her guidance counselor was going to be her foster mom—Stevie studied the fancy Victorian mansion in front of her. And that's what it was—a *mansion.* Mrs. Kirby called it a "house," but it was definitely more than that.

Beside Stevie were Hailey and Alissa, two young girls she'd just been informed were also going to be staying with Mrs. Kirby. They fidgeted and craned their necks to look around—but were absolutely silent. Stevie figured their stomachs were probably churning with the same emotions as hers: anger mixed with sprinkles of awe and heavy dollops of fear.

Eight-years-old and ten-years-old respectively, Hailey and

Alissa were extraordinarily petite. They were like little fairies, unfairly placed in a cold, unfamiliar world—one dark-haired, one strawberry blond with coke bottle thick glasses. Stevie's heart went out to them, much good as that ever did anyone. Her jaw clenched harder. Yes, Mrs. Kirby was a good person. But there was only so much even the *best* person could do, and the moment Natalie introduced Alissa and Hailey to Stevie and mentioned they were being fostered by Mrs. Kirby too, Stevie's hope withered into a blackened, stringy thing. And *that* had surprised her—that she'd actually *had* a small tender morsel of hope in the first place. Was she totally stupid or what? She'd really thought she knew better by now. She wanted to say something reassuring to Hailey and Alissa. They were quiet, cute as buttons, and *young*. They stood a chance of finding a forever home, especially compared to her, but she said nothing. Little kids weren't idiots, and from the bit Natalie said—and what she didn't say—Stevie gleaned that these two had both been in the system a while already, hence their wariness. It didn't matter how cute or sweet you were. There was no rhyme or reason to why some kids were born into love, or, at least, into families with the ability and desire to care for their offspring, while others got the opposite of those things. In fact, it was probably better—or safer, anyway—if you were a bit of an asshole like she was. At least she didn't get messed with.

Stevie realized she had clenched her fists, after all. She forced them open and tried to look chill as the big shiny red door opened. Cozy heat and warm golden light spilled into the frigid evening air. And haloed by all that light was Mrs. Kirby herself, smiling and welcoming them in like she was genuinely excited they'd arrived.

"Finally," she exclaimed. "You're here!"

Stevie smiled despite her nerves. It was such a relief to be ushered inside. A huge part of her had been sure Mrs. Kirby would change her mind, positive her question that day in her office all those weeks ago, "How would you feel about coming to live with me?" had been asked out of kindness, not any sincere desire. And yet here Stevie was, days before Christmas, walking into a house that would've been the perfect setting for a Christmas movie, carrying all her worldly possessions. She hated herself for being so weak, but honestly, even if staying with Mrs. Kirby didn't last long, it was better than the alternative—one that she knew better than to share with anyone. She was done with temporary placements and crappy group homes. There was a good chance her mom, AKA Marilyn, would show up again at some point. And if not? Well, she'd get a job or something. She had friends with street smarts—the only upside of the foster system, in her opinion. They'd help her find a place to squat until she could buy a secondhand car or something more permanent to stay in. She was only thirteen, but so what? Age was just a state of mind, right? That's what Marilyn said all the time, anyway.

"Are you going to come in, Stevie, or do you need a minute alone?"

Stevie startled. She'd done that thing that so often got her into trouble at school: disappeared into her head. She wasn't ignoring anyone or being "willfully disrespectful."

She was just—doing it again. Rats!

She swallowed and tried to speak. Nothing came out. She cleared her throat and tried again. Successfully this time. "I'll come in. Something smells really good. Thank you."

"It's roast chicken with veggies and mashed potatoes," Mrs. Kirby said as if it was no big deal. "I hope you're hungry."

Stevie was always hungry.

Dinner surprised Stevie by not being as awkward as she feared. The food was delicious—and plentiful. Mrs. Kirby, who asked them to call her Maddie, insisted they should eat as much as they wanted—and seemed to mean it. She smiled when Stevie gobbled up seconds, then thirds, of creamy potatoes with to-die-for gravy. And when Stevie asked, "Is this gravy homemade?" Maddie gave a full-on grin. "You bet. I can teach you how to make it sometime if you want."

Stevie did want that. She wanted that a lot—and even if it would never come to pass, it was very kind of Maddie to offer.

There was another girl at Mrs. Kirby's too, a fifteen-year-old named Jo, who'd arrived the night before. Jo was the type of girl that Stevie found intimidating at school: well-spoken, tall and slim, and somehow polished and put together looking, even though, at a second glance, her clothes were almost as ragged as Stevie's. She seemed nice, though—and smiled shyly at Stevie more than once, which was not how most pretty, obviously smart older girls usually reacted to her baggy jeans, gray sweatshirt, board shoe wearing self. At best, she was invisible to them. At worst—well, there was no "worst" anymore. They'd learned the hard way to leave her alone.

The rest of the evening was surprisingly comfortable too. Stevie had stayed at places where after meals, heck, *during* meals, people were as silent and expressionless as stones—and about as friendly. But Maddie was the same way in her home that she was at school. She had this gentle, no-pressure way of letting you talk or not, whatever you were more comfortable with, that Stevie appreciated, and that put them all at ease. And she told funny stories and asked interesting questions but didn't try too hard.

When no one could eat another bite, Jo offered to help with the dishes, and Stevie got up too, starting to clear plates.

Maddie insisted she didn't need any help with the dishes, saying she'd take care of them later, adding lightly that maybe there would be a chore chart or something in the future.

Stevie was crestfallen. Maybe it was dumb, but she wanted to do the dishes—wanted to give back in some little way, to not just be a total freeloader. Maddie must have sensed as much because she nodded Stevie's way. "Of course, if you really *want* to load the dishwasher, you can, but tonight's supposed to be a special treat. I don't want you to feel any pressure."

Stevie knew it was stupid, but she practically jumped up from the table.

There was something very weird and nice about doing dishes while other people chatted in a friendly, homey way. Maddie outlined possible plans for the next few days, including going shopping in town for little gifts for each other. Then she suggested, almost shyly, that it was her family's tradition—one she'd like to continue if they were game—to write letters to Santa.

Write a letter to Santa? Stevie hadn't written a letter to Santa since, well, since she was much smaller than Alissa and Hailey, put it that way.

But she felt so grateful to be in this cozy place, surrounded by greenery, twinkling lights, and not just one but *two* huge Christmas trees, that she couldn't help but get caught up in the excitement that Alissa and Hailey were obviously feeling.

As they were getting paper and picking pencils, Jo caught Stevie's eye and quirked one eyebrow the tiniest bit, not rudely and not in a making fun of Maddie way, but just enough to say, "I know, right? Pretty weird!"

And it was a bit weird, yes, but it was also just one more thing to like about Maddie. That she saw the four of them, a collection of unwanted mutts, as people who should get to do something as simple and fun as write to Santa. That she would act like there might actually be a chance, any chance at all, for the four of them to have wishes that came true.

They each settled in various parts of the house to write. Stevie chose the "family room," which, as far as Stevie could tell, was just a word you used when you had more than one "living room" and needed to distinguish between the similar spaces. Initially, the huge armchair set near a legit, 100 percent real fireplace that crackled cheerily away seemed the perfect place to jot a note. Now, however, contemplating the sheet of ivory stationery lying atop the hardcovered book she was using as a makeshift desk, Stevie wished she hadn't just loaded the dishwasher. She should've scrubbed the pots and pans too. Anything would be better than staring at a blank page.

She chewed the end of her purple pencil lightly, then caught herself and stopped. She didn't want Maddie to think she was mistreating her property.

Okay, here goes nothing, Stevie finally decided. With great resolve, she bowed her head and joined the other girls who were quietly scribbling away in various cozy spots around the big Christmas tree.

Dear Santa,

You already know who I am, but in case you've forgotten (as the jaded side of me says you obviously have), my name is Stevie Fox. I am thirteen. I am staying at Mrs. Madeline Kirby's house for a while. She's my guidance counselor at school and is the person who figured out my mom bailed (again). She didn't think it was "appropriate" for me to live alone in our apartment and called social services. Not gonna lie. It kind of pissed me off, but I get she was just doing her job. Also, rent was due, and since I had (have!) no money, I would've gotten busted anyway.

Her husband and daughter were killed in an accident. I heard some teachers talking about it at the gossip factory, aka my school. That's only relevant because it makes me think she knows how life can really suck and how there's nothing you can do about it. Also, it makes me feel like things could be worse. My mom isn't dead, after all.

Maddie (she asked us to call her that, so I'm not being disrespectful) also noticed that every foster home and group home I got stuck in sucked worse than the last one.

It's weird that I'm looking forward to Christmas this year. I'm okay if it lets me down, but I really hope it will be nice for the other girls, especially Hailey and Alissa because they're little.

Stevie contemplated her cramped handwriting, forced herself not to cross anything out, and flipped the page. Jo, who was also nestled in the family room, almost out of view beside the big Christmas tree, still seemed to be writing, so Stevie wrote some more, too.

Maddie said this thing at dinner about being grateful. It kind of freaked me out—that she would still be grateful after everything she's been through. She's a good person, and anyone who gets to stay with her long term is super lucky. I know that's not me, and I get it, but I'll try to follow her example anyway. I'm grateful that I'm here right now. I already know I'm going to be a really hard worker and that I'll be able to take care of myself, but getting to stay at Maddie's, even for a little while, is a much-needed break.

Sincerely,

Stevie Fox

P.S. Maddie says we're supposed to ask for something. I don't cook very much, but I think I would like to. Food is good—makes you grow and all that (though I'll probably always be a short dwarf), but even better, it makes me feel good. And when you eat with other people, it just feels . . . good. (I'm sorry I keep using the word "good" so much. My English teacher would definitely give me marks off for not being specific, but you're Santa and this isn't for marks, so SUCK IT, Mr. B!!!) Anyway, back to the point. I think you've eaten enough milk and cookies in your life, that you probably have a really kick-ass cookie recipe. So yeah, I would like your favorite Christmas cookie recipes. Yeah, that's right. It being Christmas, this being a wish list, I am asking for not just one cookie recipe, but all your faves. (Ha ha! I'm so greedy, hey?)

P.P.S. I totally get it if you can't share your recipes with me. No worries.

It was late when they finished their Christmas letters, so Maddie took them on a tour of the rest of the house, including their sleeping arrangements.

Even though Stevie didn't know Jo very well at all, the second-floor room Maddie chose for her seemed perfect. It looked like a study—or what she imagined a "study" to look like having only ever read about them in books. Jo looked shyly excited too, and Stevie's stomach squeezed with happiness. It was nice when something worked out.

Then Maddie showed Alissa and Hailey their bedroom, also on the second floor. She said she thought they might enjoy rooming together more than being alone in separate rooms, and from their matching smiles and the little giggle that Hailey let out, she was right.

While the other girls washed up and brushed their teeth, Maddie pulled Stevie aside. "The room I have in mind for you is on the main floor like mine."

Stevie had no idea what to expect and swallowed hard as she followed Maddie back downstairs, then toward a heavy oak door that opened just off the kitchen of all things.

Maddie's hand rested on the door's small antique knob, but she didn't open it right away. "This room is a bit . . . unique. I think it was a pantry of some kind, but that it also did double duty as a room for kitchen help or a live-in maid or something." Maddie laughed. "Not that I'm implying I expect or want you to be my maid. I just thought there was something, I don't know, sort of homey or nostalgic about the room that you, with all the reading you do, might appreciate. The bed is built into the back wall, and there's a big old apple barrel beside it—over one hundred years old. It kind of amazes me. Through all the renovations and changes in owners this house has seen, no one ever got rid of. And the room still smells softly of apples, even after all these years. Plus, there's a big built-in bureau—"

Maddie interrupted herself with a gusty inhale. "I'm talking your ear off! Just come and have a peek."

Stevie's mind reeled. She honestly would've slept on a pullout in Maddie's living room and thought herself awesomely lucky. She fully expected the "unique" room to be great because how could any space in this house not be—and yet she was still unprepared for the burst of emotions that sizzled through her when Maddie clicked on a light and Stevie followed her over the threshold. She gasped.

"Are you all right?" Genuine concern laced Maddie's voice.

Stevie could only nod. Then she felt a smile start all the way down in her belly and spread through her body with a tingle. She understood what Maddie meant; it did look like it had probably been servants' quarters at some time in history—but quarters designed by someone who had appreciated their servant, at least.

The entire space, from floor to walls to low ceiling, was constructed of gleaming, time-burnished wood. In the soft light of the overhead bulb, each crook, cranny, and surface glowed a warm welcome. On the far end of the room, which was ten steps away, if that, the built-in-bed—a nook really—that Maddie had mentioned, was made up with soft white linens, a poufy duvet (also in white), and three plump pillows.

Stevie turned slightly and there, just behind her, beside the door, was the built-in "bureau" Maddie referred to. Stevie was glad to have a name for it because she would've just called it a dresser. The mirror had gold detailing around its edges that caught the light and sparkled.

Maddie waited, expecting a comment of some kind, Stevie guessed—but she couldn't speak. Could only gawk some more, take in yet another detail.

The two walls running between the bureau and bed were not actually "walls" at all. They were floor-to-ceiling shelves. And there was the awesome apple barrel, near the head of the bed, like the most perfect bedside table ever. Stevie closed her eyes for a minute. Yes, Maddie was right. The softest hint of summer ripened apples kissed her senses. She opened her eyes again.

"This is really where you want me to stay while I'm here?"

Maddie gave her a searching look. "Is that all right?"

Stevie's face flamed. "All right? No, it's perfect. So cozy and snug and . . . " She'd been about to add *safe,* but that sounded so lame. "I . . . love it."

"Me too! I could never bring myself to change it or remodel it. The only changes this room has seen since the house was built was that someone installed a light and an electrical socket, long before my husband and me—" Maddie's voice cracked a little on the last word, and Stevie thought she knew how Maddie felt. Grief and missing a person punched extra hard sometimes, usually when you least expected it. "Anyway," Maddie continued after a breath, "I'm especially glad now that I didn't change it. It must've been meant for you all along."

The casual comment did something funny to Stevie's sinuses. She coughed and turned away from Maddie. As lovely a thought as that was—that something good could've been meant for her all along—and as much as she'd enjoyed every minute of her night here at Maddie's house, guilt suddenly soured Stevie's stomach. Wherever Marilyn was, she was definitely not having as nice a time—and whether she did a crap job of it or not, Marilyn was her mother. Wasn't Stevie meant for *her* all along?

"Um, I'm really tired. Can I go to bed now?"

"Of course, honey." Maddie's head tilted as if silently adding, "Are you okay?"

Stevie pretended she didn't notice the silent query, said thanks, and slipped back to the main entrance where her backpack and a small black garbage bag holding all her other belongings sat by her jacket and sneakers.

She had just finished brushing her teeth in the main floor's washroom when there was a light tap on the door.

"No rush at all, but do you need anything before I go up to check on Alissa, Hailey, and Jo?"

Stevie spat into the sink. "No. I'm good. Thanks."

After a moment, Maddie spoke again. "Okay, sweet dreams. See you in the morning."

Stevie carefully rinsed the white ceramic basin, making sure not one speck of toothpaste lingered. She waited until she heard Maddie's footsteps on the stairs, then slung her pack over her shoulder, scooped up the garbage bag, and eased out of the bathroom. Checking both ways, she zipped down the hall, slipped through the dining room, and found the kitchen.

Finally, she was tucked into that little room and burrowing into that crisp, clean nest of a bed. Her sinuses were still full, and her eyes were itchy and hot. She stared up at the inky blackness above her and willed away dark thoughts. Forced herself to imagine, instead, all the kinds of desserts and dishes the person who'd stayed in this room before her might have made with all those apples once stored here.

❄

Stevie stretched in the luxurious bed, loving the smooth cotton against her bare legs and reveling in the scent of coffee wafting to her room and the soft clank of dishes from whoever was already up and puttering in the kitchen. It was one of the best parts of this bedroom, the homey feeling of being included—when she wasn't even in the room yet!

Suddenly her eyes flashed open. It was Christmas morning! She was hit with very conflicting feelings: Excitement. Disappointment. She was thrilled the big day was here. She, Jo, Alissa, Hailey, and Maddie had been looking forward to it so much. The downside to its arrival, however, was a biggie. It meant, no doubt, that her time here would wrap up soon.

The last few days had been a lovely, surreal blur of shopping, baking, playing board games, and visiting with Maddie's mother, Claire. There were so many highlights that Stevie couldn't have picked any particular favorites. No wait, that was a lie. Three things did stand out.

The first occurred when Stevie helped Hailey decorate a sugar cookie, and Hailey had looked up at her with a big grin instead of her usual tentative smile. "I always wanted a big sister with hair like mine."

Her comment made Stevie choke on her cookie. Hailey's hair was a lovely strawberry blond, so soft and shiny and gently curly that she looked like a little angel. Stevie's mop was definitely more carrot than strawberry—but she didn't want to put her low self-esteem on this precious kid, so she just smiled. "I used to daydream about having sisters too."

Her words made everyone go quiet for a second. Then Jo and Alissa both exclaimed, "Me too!" at the same time. The whole table laughed.

The other really special moment wasn't a moment at all; it was a constant so wonderful it made her heart hurt even though she was happy to be a part of it. Stevie was awed by Maddie and Claire, Maddie's mother, and couldn't help but watch them. They were like some really funny, really heart-warming, really educational TV show or something. She didn't have any experience with other adult daughter/mother relationships, and she didn't know if Maddie and Claire were the norm or what, but studying them made her think. She hadn't been enough for her mom obviously, and/or, one could argue, her mom was bad at the whole parenting thing. But in her mom's defense, Marilyn had never had anyone like Claire around to love her either. That was what was so cool about Maddie and Claire. You could see their love for each other, even when they were teasing each other—maybe especially then. For as long as Stevie had been with Marilyn, it was always just the two of them. She couldn't help but wonder. . . . Maybe if Marilyn had someone like Claire in her life, things would have gone really differently than they had. But that was too sad for Christmas.

Stevie popped out of bed and smoothed down the beautiful flannel nightie Maddie had given her the night before. Feeling like a little kid, she bounced into the kitchen to help prep a breakfast feast to enjoy after gift opening.

"Merry Christmas!" Hailey and Alissa yelled the second they entered the room, making her grin.

"Merry Christmas, weirdos," she muttered back—and everyone laughed. It made her feel silly and warm inside. Instead of side eying her, they seemed to totally get her sense of humor.

"Perfect timing!" Maddie announced. "Let's open presents."

Stevie was touched by Hailey's gift: a little notebook with a fox on its front cover. Even more adorable was Hailey's shy whisper, "I thought you'd like it because of your name. Get it?"

"I *do* get it. Good one," Stevie whispered back, "and I love it. Thank you."

Stevie immediately knew what she was going to use it for:

writing out any recipes or cooking instructions Maddie gave her, so she could keep them always.

Jo had gotten her a little gift too: a rechargeable flashlight. The others seemed mildly surprised by the gift, murmuring, "Oh, nice . . ." in a not quite convincing way as if relieved Jo hadn't gotten them flashlights. But Stevie laughed with loud, surprised delight—at the gift, but also at the bubbly glee rising up in her. She and Jo had an inside joke! She'd read about inside jokes before but had never had one. The first thing Jo said when she saw Stevie's wonderful room their first morning was, "It's perfect, but you need a light to read in bed!"

After the last gift was opened, they all galloped back to the kitchen and did the final work toward their Christmas breakfast feast. And that was highlight number three. Stevie loved every minute of being directed by Maddie about how to do this or mix that, and she was beyond thrilled when Maddie asked if she could follow a recipe.

"I think so, yeah," she said—and Maddie got her to make blueberry waffles all by herself! The chore took on even more special significance when she discovered that blueberry waffles for Christmas brunch were part of Maddie and her husband and daughter's holiday tradition.

Later that night, while everybody played with their gifts and visited some more, Stevie replayed the day, recalling each moment in as much detail as possible, wanting to commit it all to memory, so she could pull it out again and again in the future. It wasn't the gifts that made the day so special. It wasn't even the food. It was that she'd never been surrounded by people who were so happy to be together. Even when she was quiet, lost in her thoughts from time to time—or the others were—it felt like they all belonged. And suddenly, just like that, it was too much.

Stevie needed to be alone. She asked Maddie if she could go sit on the porch for a bit.

"Of course. Let me get you a blanket."

Stevie hadn't been outside in the big wicker rocking chair for long when Maddie joined her, two cups of hot chocolate in hand.

"I know the last thing you probably want right now is something else to eat, but I thought hot chocolate out on the porch, surrounded by the crispy snow and the stars above, felt extra Christmassy."

Stevie smiled. It really did.

"Also, I wanted to check in with you. It's been such a wonderful Christmas for me, but it feels bittersweet too. I wondered if it's the same for you."

Stevie nodded. That was the thing about Maddie—why she was so loved not only by her but by all the kids at school. She just . . . got you.

"I don't know." Stevie gestured at the big house behind her, its windows glowing with Christmas lights and shadows of its happy occupants flitting past here and there. "This is all so great, but it also sucks, you know?"

Maddie nodded.

"Part of me feels awful having fun when my mom probably isn't . . . and when, like, I don't know where she is."

"I get that."

"She's not a totally bad person, you know. She's not."

Maddie nodded again. "I know."

"And when you asked if I would like to live with you and I said yes, I meant it. I really did. But I also know it's not possible."

Maddie's head tilted as if Stevie's last comment confused her. She sank onto a bench beside the wicker rocking chair and pulled a piece of Stevie's blanket over her lap.

"What do you mean 'not possible?'"

"Just that, well . . ." For a second, Stevie couldn't find the words, but then she spoke in a rush. "Jo, Alissa, Hailey . . . They don't have moms. They don't have families. They're free to live here with you forever if that's what you all want. But that's not how it is for me."

Maddie looked down and was uncharacteristically quiet for a long time.

Here it comes, thought Stevie. I'm right. My mom's already shown up again, or Natalie's told Maddie I have to go back to a group home or something because I have a parent. Maddie probably just wanted to spare me the bad news until after Christmas because, of course, she's nice like that.

Finally, Maddie spoke. "When I asked if you wanted to live with me, Stevie, I wasn't just asking out the blue. I'd already asked Natalie how it would work and if it would be possible—not because I care whether the arrangements will be difficult—no matter how difficult they are, I'll see them through—but because I didn't want to disappoint you again. You've already had enough disappointments for a whole lifetime, and then some."

Stevie tucked her half of the blanket around herself a little more tightly and waited for it. "But?" she asked.

"No buts. For as long as your mom is not here, this is your home. And if, *when*, your mom shows up again, we'll take it from there. If you need—or want—to live with her again, I want you to know you'll always have a home here with me too."

"Really?" It sounded to Stevie like Maddie was saying that she was going to be there for her from here on out, no matter what—that it didn't matter what the details were. Everything would just be okay. Maddie would always watch out for her.

She hadn't realized she'd expressed that thought aloud until Maddie squeezed her shoulder and said, "Yes, that's exactly what I mean. You got it."

Stevie had watched a lot of Christmas specials on TV. She'd sang Christmas carols and heard a zillion of them on the radio. She'd read countless books containing Christmas "themes" as Mr. B. would say, but until that moment, she'd never understood how truly merry and perfect—and life-changing—a Christmas really could be.

"I'm . . . I'm just going to sit out here a little while longer," Stevie said.

"You bet. Take all the time you need." Maddie got to her feet—and was almost at the door when Stevie whispered, "Maddie?"

"Yeah?"

Stevie swallowed against the hard lump in her throat. "Thank you," she whispered.

"Aw, sweetie . . . you're so welcome. Merry Christmas."

ALISSA MANN

AUTHOR TESS THOMPSON

This was not how her life was supposed to go.

Alissa wasn't supposed to be in a social worker's office that smelled of burned coffee on a cold night in December. Alone. Without Mommy and Daddy. *Please wake up,* she thought. *Let this be a bad dream.*

But dreams didn't have smells. Nightmares were over faster than this. If she called out from her cozy bed in their warm house, her mother came. Not now. Her mother was dead. She would never comfort Alissa in the middle of the night ever again.

The social worker, Mrs. Keele, had left her in the office to wait while she wrapped up some details. Alissa didn't know what details meant, only that she was to be sent to a foster home because her mother and father were dead.

Shaking, she pulled her sweater tighter around her middle. She'd had her jacket on after her school concert, but she didn't now. Where had her jacket gone? A space heater in the corner made a humming insect sound but no heat warmed the room. Her tired, puffy eyes stung. A split in the orange plastic cushion of the chair dug into her leg as she looked around the small office. Layers of paper and folders littered a grey metal desk. A calendar with a photograph of kittens playing with a ball of string hung on the wall behind the desk.

The scent of burned coffee reminded her of the time her mother forgot to turn the electric pot off, and the stench had filled the house. Daddy had teased Mommy, saying she was an absentminded professor. This was their joke because they were both professors and equally forgetful. They'd never forgotten Alissa though. She'd been their whole world. Hadn't Mommy just said that to her last week?

The accident had been at night, coming home from her school holiday recital. Her fourth-grade class had sung "Frosty the Snowman." Alissa was the smallest in her class, so the teacher had put her on the bottom rung of the bleachers. Her parents had been in the front row with their video camera. They'd smiled and clapped extra hard when the song finished.

Going home, the roads were icy. Daddy said not to worry. He was a great driver even with ice because he was extra careful because of the precious cargo he carried. "That's us," Mommy said, as she glanced back at Alissa.

A car had lurched into their lane like a bumper car ride at the county fair they'd been to last summer. She remembered that. Mommy screamed. Then, everything went black. Alissa woke up in a hospital bed. Her head and body ached. Her mouth so dry. A nurse with hair like a mushroom and creases in her cheeks had given her ice-cold water in a plastic cup with a bendy straw. "Where's my mommy and daddy?" she'd asked.

The nurse with the mushroom hair zipped her lips together and avoided eye contact, then scurried away. A policeman in a blue uniform and a round stomach came to talk to her. He'd spoken softly, like they were at the library.

Her parents hadn't survived the accident. "They were killed instantly," he said. "They didn't suffer."

"But I heard Mommy scream," Alissa said.

The rims of the police officer's eyes turned pink. "I'm sorry, Alissa."

She was an orphan now. She asked him what would happen to her. He said social services would come. "They'll find a place for you to go," he said.

"A place?"

"A home with a family. A foster home," he said. "Or, a relative who wants you."

There was no one. Her parents were only children. Alissa's grandparents had all died before she was born. Mommy had once told her that she and Daddy had been drawn to each other because of their similar experiences, having lost their single mothers young. "We became each other's family," she'd said.

So, that meant she would go to a foster home. She'd heard of those. A girl in her grade had been in one. She came to school in dirty, ragged clothes, and her eyes reminded Alissa of a dog's eyes she'd seen in an advertisement for a pet rescue society, haunted and defeated. Mommy had once said that it was a special type of person who would offer their home to a child in need. Was she now a child in need? She didn't want to be.

Now, she waited for Mrs. Keele to return and tell her where she would go next. The vastness of that question made her chest burn. She would not go back to her own house with her pink room and unicorn pillows. She would no longer wake to the smell of bacon and pancakes. She would no longer fall asleep after a bedtime story. They'd only been halfway through the Harry Potter series. Would she ever know what happened to Harry, Ron and Hermione?

"We've done a search and there's no one in either of your parents' families that are available to take you," Mrs. Keele had said.

"I know," Alissa had replied. She could have told Mrs.

Keele that, but no one asked her anything. They just set her aside like leftover Chinese food going bad in the back of the refrigerator.

"We'll find a nice family for you," Mrs. Keele had said, as her large hands moved papers around her desk. Her skin looked chapped, and her cuticles red and irritated. Alissa wanted to offer some of Mommy's lotions that she'd always carried in her purse. Where was Mommy's purse? Had it been thrown from the car? Was it out on the highway somewhere? Were Mommy's friends sending texts to a phone that would never be picked up again?

Mommy and Daddy.

Tears came. Alissa tried to stop them, but it was useless. Grief filled her, pushing away everything but the awful bleak hopelessness. She hugged her knees and sobbed. A terrible darkness lived in her chest now. She was lost, adrift. Alone. Mrs. Keele said she couldn't go back to school. She'd no longer be best friends with Sophie. Probably that horrible Roxanne would worm her way in and become Sophie's new best friend. She'd never see Mrs. Johnson, her favorite teacher, ever again.

Everyone she loved was gone.

What would happen to their Christmas tree? There were presents under there too. Who would take them? The shell frame she'd made at school for Mommy and Daddy was under there, wrapped in sparkly blue paper. What would happen to it? And what about all their things?

Her thoughts were interrupted by Mrs. Keele's return. "Time to go, dear."

Go? Where?

Alissa was in Mrs. Kirby's kitchen. Gingerbread cookies were stacked on a platter shaped like Santa. Alissa had been allowed to have a cookie even though they hadn't yet had dinner. The sweetness remained in her mouth even after taking a sip of milk.

They'd chatted for a few minutes, then Mrs. Kirby told her something surprising.

"I knew your dad," Mrs. Kirby said. "He was a wonderful man."

"You knew him?"

"Yes, my late husband worked with him at the university. They were both professors. I remember when you were born. Your dad was so proud. He went around the whole department handing out cigars."

"Cigars?" Alissa wrinkled her nose.

"That's just something people do when a baby is born," Mrs. Kirby said. "Silly, isn't it?"

"Kind of."

"Would you like to call me Maddie, instead of Mrs. Kirby?"

"I guess so." Alissa studied Maddie. She had long dark lashes and wore pink lipstick. Her perfume smelled like a meadow of wildflowers. She wore a zebra print dress and long black boots with a heel. Mommy would have liked her. She would have complimented her boots. "Did you know my mom too?"

"Yes. I met her a few times at parties. She was very pretty and smart..." Maddie trailed off, and fidgeted with a napkin.

Alissa nodded and tried not to cry. Her Mommy had been the prettiest woman in the whole world.

They didn't suffer.

"They died," she said.

"I know, sweetie. I'm so very sorry. It hurts, doesn't it?"

"Yes," she whispered. "I just want to go home."

Maddie put her hand on Alissa's shoulder. The gentle touch made her want to crawl onto Maddie's lap and bury her face into the soft, sweet-smelling shoulder. "My husband died a few years back," Maddie continued. "My little daughter too."

A dart of shock coursed through Alissa. Did Maddie have the dark hole in her chest too? Was that what made her eyes sad?

"They were in a car accident too," Maddie said.

"Oh." She couldn't think what to say.

"I know how hard it is to understand what happened but I'm here to help."

"You have sad eyes," Alissa said.

"Yes, I do," Maddie said. "My heart's sad, so it shows in my eyes. I'm here for you now. The others will be too. Your new sisters. You won't ever have to be alone again."

Alissa's mind tumbled over this idea. Would her sisters become new friends? Other girls who understood what it was like to be without parents?

"I know I can't take the place of your parents, but I'll love you like my own."

"Why?"

"Because loving you makes it hurt less that my daughter is in heaven instead of here with me."

Maddie seemed nice—and she'd always wanted a sister. Not this way, of course, but her parents were gone. "I'd like to have sisters."

Maddie smiled and kissed the top of Alissa's head. "I have something for you." She went to the counter where a blue purse sat next to the telephone. Maddie reached inside, and returned to the table to set a small silver heart in front of Alissa. "Whenever you feel scared or anxious, hold this heart and know your mother and father are now your guardian angels. They'll always be with you, even if you can't see them."

Alissa squeezed her fingers around the cold metal. Seconds later, warmth spread through her body, seemingly radiating from the heart. For the first time, she had hope that she would be all right. Her mother and father were her angels now. All she had to do was remember them, and they would be with her.

"Thank you," she said to Maddie, remembering her manners. Mommy always said there was always something to be thankful for, even during the darkest times. She was thankful for Maddie Kirby.

Please, Mommy and Daddy, look over me and this nice lady. And my new sisters.

Alissa was seated at the dining room table in Maddie's house with three other girls. She couldn't yet think of them as her sisters even though she felt an instant connection with them. They all had sad eyes too. Still, they were strangers, thrown together because their parents were gone. Jo was a big girl of fifteen, with green eyes that were angry, as well as wretched. When Alissa smiled at her, Jo looked away and flushed. Stevie was the next oldest at thirteen, with a face kind of like a storm cloud. Her hair was the color of a copper cup Alissa's father used to drink Moscow Mules out of on Saturday nights. The littlest girl, Hailey, wore thick glasses and darted glances at Alissa with her big blue eyes. She was so tiny and thin that Alissa thought she might float away like a balloon if someone didn't hold her down. With that in mind, she scooted her chair closer and reached under the table to take Hailey's hand.

Hailey squeezed her hand back and they exchanged a smile.

Maddie set a pile of blank paper on the table. "Since we're so close to Christmas, I thought it would be fun to write Santa a letter."

Alissa glanced around the table. The two older girls

looked down at their laps. A tear caught in Hailey's lower lashes.

Alissa had planned to ask for the Barbie camper. Now everything was different. All she wanted was her mother and father to come get her. She'd give up Christmas presents for the rest of her life if that could happen. But even Santa couldn't deliver that wish.

Maddie smiled at her. "He knows you've been through a lot and that you've been a good girl."

"Okay," Alissa said. "I'll write one."

Maddie passed around paper and pencils for everyone. The girls dispersed from the table, wandering to other places in the house. Alissa chewed on the end of her pencil, debating about what to write. Last month, she and Mommy had kept gratitude journals. Every day they wrote something they were thankful for and then shared it on the way to school. "No matter how bad things are," Mommy's voice echoed through her mind. "There is always something to be thankful for."

Alissa didn't want to be thankful just at the moment. She wanted to scream and cry and break things. Yet, Mommy was right. She was here with Maddie and the other girls. The house was warm and pretty with two enormous sparkly trees. The room smelled of cookies and hot cocoa. Maddie had managed to bring her clothes, books and dolls from home. They were already arranged in the upstairs bedroom she would share with Hailey.

Dear Santa,

I'm thankful for my new home even though I miss Mommy and Daddy. I'd still like the Barbie camper even though it seems stupid now. I wonder if Barbie's parents are alive? I've never seen them so maybe they're dead too. If that's true, does she have a foster mom like me? I'd also like you to bring something for each of my new sisters that will make them smile and take away their sad eyes.

Yours truly,

Alissa Mann

That night, after they were allowed to eat a sugar cookie and drink a glass of milk, Alissa brushed her teeth. She stared back at her reflection, feeling almost as if her body and face belonged to someone else. Would she ever feel normal again?

She slipped between the covers in her new twin bed. Across from her, Hailey did the same. Maddie tucked the covers up around her shoulders, and kissed her forehead, just like Mommy did. Then, she did the same for Hailey.

"Will you be all right with just the night light?" Maddie asked.

Alissa nodded.

Hailey said, "Yes, ma'am."

"My daughter was afraid of the dark," Maddie said, as she perched on the end of Alissa's bed. "I bought the brightest light I could find. In the morning, I would come in and she'd have turned on the lamp anyway."

"Did she get in trouble?" Hailey asked.

"No. I always figured there were more things to worry about than whether or not she needed the lights on," Maddie said. "Anyway, you girls sleep well. In the morning, we'll do a little Christmas shopping, and go to the holiday festival at the town center."

"Really?" Hailey asked. "I've never been before."

"It's one of the best parts of Christmas," Maddie said.

Alissa squeezed her eyes shut to keep from crying. She and her parents had gone there every holiday season. They'd bought a new ornament each year for their tree. What would happen to all those ornaments now?

"What is it, sweetie?" Maddie asked.

"What happened to all the ornaments at my house?" Alissa asked.

Maddie swept a hand through her silky brown hair. "Your mommy's best friend is taking care of putting away your parents' things for you to have when you're older. I'll make sure she puts those in a safe place, okay?"

Alissa's body flooded with relief. "Thank you, Maddie."

"You're welcome. Good night, loves."

Maddie went to the doorway and turned off the overhead light. "Door open or closed?" she asked.

"Open," Hailey and Alissa said at the same time.

"Open, it is then," Maddie said. With one last smile, she disappeared from the doorway.

Alissa heard her footsteps down the hall, and then a murmuring of voices as she stopped in Jo's room. She lay on her back looking up at the ceiling. At home, her mother had placed glowing stars on the ceiling. Here, there was nothing but black. After a few minutes, the sound of Hailey crying startled her from her thoughts.

"Hailey," she whispered. "Are you all right?"

"No," Hailey said in a shaky voice. "I'm scared."

"It's all right," Alissa said. "I'm here."

"Would you sleep next to me?" she asked. "Just for a few minutes."

"Sure." Alissa scooted out of the covers and crossed the few feet to the other bed. They were both small enough to fit nicely in the bed, laying on their backs and holding hands.

"Sometimes when I can't sleep, I tell myself stories," Hailey said. "I have one about a Dachshund puppy. Would you like to hear it?"

"Sure. I love dogs," Alissa said. A feeling she'd never had before washed over her. She wanted to protect her little friend, her new sister, from harm and further pain. Not that she had any idea how. Maybe listening to her story was a good start.

"Once upon a time, there was a dog named Zeke," Hailey said.

Her new sister only got out two more sentences before she drifted off to sleep. Alissa slipped back to her own bed, and curled on her side. The house creaked. Maddie's footsteps, as she prepared for Christmas downstairs, soothed Alissa. She heard Mommy's voice in her head. *Everything will be all right, my darling. One day at a time.*

Eventually, she fell asleep and dreamed of angels singing "Silent Night."

HAILEY KIRBY

AUTHOR JUDITH KEIM

Hailey Bennett sat in the cozy kitchen wondering how to begin. Mrs. Kirby, her new foster mother, had asked her and the other three girls in the house to write a letter to Santa. She tapped the pencil against the wooden tabletop, trying to form the words in her head.

She'd learned at school that writing words was easier for her than talking. Talking sometimes got her into big trouble. Besides, she liked the words and people she made up and kept inside her head. These characters all lived in fancy big houses with a Mom and a Dad who loved them. Not in houses where yelling and hitting took place. Her teacher told her she had a great imagination and that someday she could become an excellent storyteller. Maybe. Now, she'd better pretend she believed in Santa. She looked around. The other girls were busy writing to him. She wondered if she could make the words come out right.

She began to form the printed letters on paper as carefully as she could.

"Dear Santa, I want a pupy for Xmas with lots of kisses.

Your frind,

Hailey Bennett."

"How are you doing, sweetheart? Need any help?" Mrs. Kirby asked, coming into the kitchen and giving her a friendly smile.

Hailey shook her head. She knew better than to bring attention to herself. That had only caused a slap or a nasty remark in the foster home she'd just left. Those people were called out of town for the holidays to take care of a sick relative. Or so the person from Foster Care Services told her. They'd left without even saying goodbye to her. Another house that didn't work for her.

At the memory of finding herself alone again, tears escaped her eyes and dropped onto the lenses of her eyeglasses. She quickly took them off and rubbed them dry. She didn't want the other girls to see. They might call her a crybaby, like the kids at school sometimes did. Or "four-eyes," which was almost as bad.

Hailey left the kitchen and joined the older girls in the family room. Carefully, so as not to draw attention to herself, she sat on the floor by the doorway. From here, she wouldn't bother anyone. It was a good place to make up some of her favorite stories. At eight, she'd lived through a lot of disappointments, and these stories brought her comfort.

Hailey studied the lights on the Christmas tree and listened to the holiday music. Soon she became lost in a memory of colorful lights, a soft voice, and blue eyes. She'd been told her mother had died when she was four, and they didn't know how to find her father. She thought it must be a mistake. Somewhere her mother was looking for her. She was sure of it. When she got old enough, she'd go find her.

Mrs. Kirby came and sat down beside her. She had long brown hair and dark-brown eyes. Kind eyes. "Pretty Christmas lights, huh?"

Hailey nodded.

"I hope you'll be comfortable here with me and the other girls. Anytime you need to talk to me about something, feel free to do it. Okay?"

Hailey studied her and then nodded. This new foster mother seemed really nice, but only time would tell if this house would be the right one.

"I have something for you," Mrs. Kirby said. "Something to welcome you."

Hailey felt her eyes widen. This was something new.

"Would you like to open it now?" Mrs. Kirby's eyes sparkled with excitement.

Her pulse speeding up with excitement she didn't dare show, Hailey bobbed her head up and down.

Mrs. Kirby got to her feet, went into her downstairs bedroom, and returned with a gaily-wrapped package. "Here. This is for you."

Hailey accepted the gift and held it to her chest. "Mine?"

"Yes, yours," Mrs. Kirby said, patting her shoulder. "Go ahead and open it."

Hailey carefully unwrapped the package, slowly lifted the paper off, and stared with disbelief at the stuffed puppy dog. The brown fur felt soft as she lifted it into her arms. Dark-brown, button eyes stared deep inside her to where she hid her feelings. The pink-felt tongue sewn into the mouth looked as if it wanted to kiss her.

"Mine?" Hailey said again, needing to be sure. It was the closest she'd ever come to having something like this of her own.

"Yes, sweetie, it's yours. Later, after the holidays, we'll get a real dog in the house. But all of us will have to decide together on what kind it'll be."

Hailey buried her face into the puppy's soft fur and felt her eyes fill. This time, words inside her head weren't enough. "I … I love it," she managed to say. Her lips trembled with emotion.

Hailey noticed Mrs. Kirby's eyes grow as watery as her own. "This dog will help you. Any time you feel uncomfortable, Hailey, bring him to me, and we'll talk to him and you about it. Okay?"

Hailey thought for a moment, and nodded, trying not to be a big crybaby.

Throughout the rest of the evening, Hailey held the dog close to her.

One of the girls saw her and asked, "What's your puppy's name?"

Hailey shrugged, too shy to answer.

"How about Charlie, for Charlie Brown?"

Hailey giggled and nodded. "Okay."

She hugged the dog. *Hi, Charlie.*

Hailey spent the next few days taking in every detail of her new surroundings and studying the other girls, Charlie constantly in tow. By now, Hailey knew the oldest girl was a dark-haired girl named Jo. The other two were Alissa, a girl not much bigger than she who had big brown eyes, and red-haired Stevie. As Mrs. Kirby explained, they'd all been in need of a new home too. Hailey studied them and held onto her dog, wondering what life would be like here. Already, it might be the best ever.

Some things might take her a while to get used to though. Like how tonight Mrs. Kirby took her hand after dinner and cheerily announced, "Time for a bath and to get ready for bed."

Hailey wasn't used to someone holding her hand. Not in a nice way.

Mrs. Kirby led her upstairs, chatting quietly about the good day they'd had. Hailey was sharing a room with Alissa. Mrs. Kirby, or Maddie as one of the big girls called her, had figured the two of them, as the youngest, wouldn't mind sharing, that it would be nice for them to know they weren't alone. Hailey was glad. She clutched Charlie to her chest, glad, too, she had Charlie to make her feel safe.

Okay, Charlie, bath time.

Upstairs, Mrs. Kirby led her into a big room at the front of the house. Though it was getting dark outside, Hailey could see the soft glow of street lights through the large window that gave a nice view of the pretty neighborhood.

Hailey noticed Mrs. Kirby looking around the room sadly, and reached out and touched her hand.

Mrs. Kirby's eyes widened and then filled with tears. She knelt on the floor and wrapped her arms around Hailey, filling her with a warm feeling. "Ah, Hailey, you're such a sweetie. I hope you're going to be happy here."

Wanting to please Mrs. Kirby, Hailey nodded, though she was waiting to be told she'd have to move. Again.

Mrs. Kirby rose and patted her on the head. "I have another surprise. Here is your new Christmas nightgown. All the girls got them."

Hailey stared at the red flannel nightgown whose collar and cuffs were edged in lace. It was beautiful. "Mine?" she asked, touching the soft, warm fabric.

"Yes, yours, Hailey. After your bath, we'll put it on and hopefully I'll have time for a short story with you and Alissa before I need to get the other girls settled."

In a daze of disbelief, Hailey took her bath, put on her new nightgown, and climbed into her soft, clean bed, the one closest to the window. Alissa, a nice girl who sometimes let her hold her unicorn pillow, slept in the other bed. She liked having Alissa in the same room.

After both girls were tucked in, Mrs. Kirby sat down on the edge of Hailey's bed with a couple of books. Hailey grinned at Alissa. Of all the things that would make this day even more magical it was having a story read to them.

As Mrs. Kirby read aloud a book about a moon and another story about a girl moving to a new home, a peace settled inside Hailey. She had a new home too.

The next day, Mrs. Kirby surprised her by saying, "We're going shopping so you can get gifts for the other girls in the house. It's Christmas Eve, and we don't have much time for you to choose something for them and get it wrapped."

Hailey simply stared at her. She'd never bought a gift or wrapped a gift or even thought of Christmas this way.

"If you've never done this before, that's okay!" said Mrs. Kirby. "I'll help you decide what to get if you need me to. Don't worry, it's going to be fun. This is what Christmas is all about—thinking of others, having fun, and remembering to be grateful for all you have."

Hailey forced words out of her head into her mouth. "Thank you. That will be fun."

Mrs. Kirby smiled. "I think so too."

Later, at the store, Hailey squeezed a five-dollar bill in her hand and hugged Charlie closer to her. The store was alive with activity as people strolled the aisles, and Christmas music played through loudspeakers. Nearby, Mrs. Kirby said, "Remember, choose something you think each of the girls would like. Something you might like yourself, perhaps. I know you've just met them, but knowing you, I'm sure you'll come up with something special for each of them."

Hailey had studied each of the girls in the house. Some choices would be easy. Some not. Charlie would help her.

It took her no time to choose a book for Alissa. She'd loved their story time as much as Hailey. For Stevie, she finally chose a notebook with a picture of a fox on it. Stevie seemed to have words in her head too. Jo was the hardest choice of all. She seemed tough, but Hailey knew better. She walked slowly up one aisle of the store and down another and then stopped in front of the hair ribbons and bows. Even though she knew Jo might be surprised, Hailey picked out a bright red bow with sparkly fake diamonds on it. It was the most beautiful bow in the store.

Satisfied, she showed Mrs. Kirby her selections.

"Perfect," she said to her. "Lovely ideas."

Brimming with pleasure, Hailey handed the lady at checkout her money and put the gifts down.

"Somebody is going to have a nice Christmas," the lady said, smiling at her.

Hailey nodded. *My sisters.* Even thinking the word sister made Hailey's heart pound with excitement, and nervousness too. It was all so new.

At home, Hailey and Mrs. Kirby worked together wrapping the gifts in Mrs. Kirby's bedroom where they had privacy. The pretty green paper and shiny silver bows seemed like gifts of their own. Hailey did her best to make the paper not so crinkly and to stick the bow in exactly the right place.

Mrs. Kirby handed her the name tags. "Okay, now you need to add these. One for each of the girls. I've printed them carefully so you can read them."

Hailey proudly attached the name tags to the right gifts. She couldn't wait to see if the girls liked them.

She carefully carried them into the living room and placed them under the tree.

"Don't look, Charlie!" She hid the stuffed dog behind her back.

Mrs. Kirby smiled at her. "Tomorrow is going to be so much fun. Now let's see how the other girls are doing with icing the cookies they made earlier."

When they walked into the large kitchen, Alissa, Stevie,

and Jo were standing around the kitchen island exclaiming over the cookies.

"Stevie's are the best," Jo said, and nobody disagreed. Hers were gorgeous, with a few extra touches on the Christmas trees and on Santa's face.

"Did you save a couple of cookies for Hailey to ice, like I asked?" Mrs. Kirby said.

Jo nodded. "Here, Hailey, these are yours."

Hailey swallowed hard. "Mine?"

"Yes. They're yours. Here's the icing and here is the spreader. Go to it," Jo said.

A few moments later, Hailey stood back. The green and red colors weren't exactly where she'd wanted them—they sort of blended too much—but the cookies were beautiful just the same.

"Go ahead and lick the spoon. We left some for you," said Mrs. Kirby.

The sugary taste on Hailey's tongue was delicious. "Mmm," she murmured, bringing a knowing smile to Mrs. Kirby's face.

Christmas morning, Alissa jumped out of bed. "Get up, sleepyhead! It's Christmas!"

Hailey's eyes flew open. It had just been moments ago that she lay awake wondering if Christmas was ever going to come. She scrambled out of bed and raced after Alissa.

Downstairs, Mrs. Kirby was in the living room with Jo and Stevie.

"Merry Christmas, girls! Come join us."

They sat together around the Christmas tree. Hailey stared at the number of brightly wrapped packages with awe. She'd never lived in a house where there were so many.

"Let's take turns opening gifts," said Mrs. Kirby.

Watching the girls open her presents for them, Hailey felt warm inside. They'd each liked her gift. She could tell. Stevie even understood why she'd chosen a notebook with a fox on it. Her last name was Fox.

And when she opened her own gifts, she almost squealed with delight. Colored pencils, pens, a notebook with a picture of a Dachshund on it, a drawing pad, and not one, but two books were hers. The notebook even had her name printed on it in big black letters.

Charlie, it's the best Christmas ever. Maybe there really is a Santa Claus.

She'd always remember this day—the music, the lights on the tree, the sound of crinkling paper, the cries of surprise. She studied Mrs. Kirby laughing with the other girls and felt as if she was in a dream.

Mrs. Kirby leaned over and gave her a kiss on the cheek. "We all have so much to be thankful for."

Yes, Charlie, you and me. Hailey hugged him hard, her eyes filling with tears of joy.

EPILOGUE: FIFTEEN YEARS LATER

SOUL SISTERS AT CEDAR MOUNTAIN LODGE

Maddie hummed a Christmas tune as she brought the last of the grocery bags in and set them on the kitchen counter. Making holiday goodies for her girls always put her in a good mood, and she danced around the kitchen as she put things away and prepared to begin her marathon baking session. In a few days, she'd be surrounded by her brood, and her heart was filled to overflowing with the anticipation.

She always looked forward to Christmas and having all the girls back home to celebrate with her, but this year was especially exciting. Alissa was getting married on Christmas Eve, and everyone had planned to spend the entire holiday week together at nearby Cedar Mountain Lodge to celebrate the family's first wedding and partake in the holiday festivities.

Maddie's cell phone rang as she pulled her rolling pin from its usual spot in the pantry, and she smiled to hear Alissa's customized ring tone playing "Here Comes the Bride."

"Hi, honey! How's our bride today?" Maddie answered with a cheery tone, but her smile faltered when she heard Alissa crying on the other end of the line.

"Mom, the wedding's off."

Uh-oh. Can the magic of the season restore the family's faith in love? Come and join Maddie, Hailey, Stevie, and Jo as they gather with Alissa at the Cedar Mountain Lodge for a holiday reunion they'll never forget.

Get the rest of the series now!

Book 2: Christmas Kisses by Judith Keim

Book 3: Christmas Wishes by Tammy L. Grace

Book 4: Christmas Hope by Violet Howe

Book 5: Christmas Dreams by Ev Bishop

Book 6: Christmas Rings by Tess Thompson

And join the authors in the Soul Sisters Chat Facebook group for book discussions, activities, and interaction with other book lovers.

CONTINUE THE STORY...

CHRISTMAS KISSES BY JUDITH KEIM, CHAPTER 1

Hailey Kirby sat in the Granite Ridge, Idaho, library on a small wooden chair in the middle of a circle of wide-eyed three-to-six-year-old children sitting on the plush, new, green carpet in the children's section. Story time was her favorite activity of her job as assistant librarian and director of children's programs, and she loved to make it as exciting as possible by acting out the characters with different voices and mannerisms.

Though their town was small, the two-story, red-brick library building was an important part of the community. It had become a gathering place for various activities. Volunteer groups used the conference room for meetings, and the book club, which had started as a small group, had grown large enough to meet there every month, filling the largest room. Best of all, the library was a place that introduced the joys of reading to children.

As she leafed through the book she was reading aloud, she studied the pictures carefully—pictures drawn by her own hand. That was something very few people knew. As part of her contract with a well-known children's book publisher, Hailey, writing and illustrating under the name of Lee Merriweather, had demanded anonymity. After lengthy discussions and with the help of her sister, Jo, acting as her lawyer, she finally won. She knew, though, as Lee Merriweather's popularity grew, she would eventually be exposed. Maybe by then, she'd be more comfortable about people knowing who she really was.

"What's Charlie going to do now?" asked one of the children, giving her a worried look.

"Is he going to get into trouble again?" another child asked.

Hailey held up a finger. "Let's see. Shall we?" One of the main characters in her stories was a boy named Charlie. He and his three friends found themselves in all kinds of trouble as they learned one life lesson after another. Each book had a happy ending, of course, because she understood how important they were.

Hailey read:

"Charlie's mother hugged him tight. "I'm so glad you came home. I missed you."

"I promise not to run away again," said Charlie. He hadn't been gone long. After going only one block with his dachshund, Zeke, he wished he hadn't done it. Like his mother had told him, "Home is where the heart is", and he knew his home was with her and the rest of his family."

"I'm glad Charlie went home," said a little girl named Regan, whom Hailey adored.

"Me, too," said Hailey. She'd found a home with Maddie Kirby when she was eight years old and would do anything in the world to repay her. It was one reason she'd come back to Granite Ridge after college. If Mom ever needed her, she'd be there in a heartbeat.

She helped the children replace their chairs at the tables set aside for them in the children's corner and checked her watch. She had just a few more hours until it was time for her to go home to pack for her stay with her family at the Cedar Mountain Lodge. She was both excited and saddened by the idea.

Alissa, her sister, had been dumped by her fiancé, Jed, days before their Christmas Eve wedding. Alissa told everyone in the family to go ahead with plans to spend time at the lodge. Travel arrangements had already been made for those flying in, the lodge had accommodations for them all, and her ex fiancé, the rat, could very well find other arrangements for the holiday. In an effort to cheer her and continue their family tradition of spending the holidays together, Hailey, her sisters, and their mom all agreed to keep to those plans. But Hailey ached for her sister. Jed had seemed the perfect man for her, and he'd disappointed them all.

Hailey spent time speaking to parents as they picked up their children from story time. She accepted hugs from all the children, loving the feel of their little arms around her.

When Nick Hensley entered the room, her pulse sputtered and kicked into a sprint. With his black, curly hair, brown eyes, and strong physique, he was beyond a hottie. The black ski jacket he wore stretched across his broad chest as if it had been made especially for him.

"Hi, Hailey. I'm here for Regan," Nick announced, looking around. "Where is she?" He sometimes helped his sister, Stacy, take care of Regan when she was too busy at the candy store in town to pick her up herself.

"Here! I'm here!" Laughing, Regan poked her head from behind a corner of the book shelf and ran to him, her arms open wide, her pink snow jacket flying behind her dark curls.

He swung her up in his arms and hugged her to him. "Okay, monkey, time to go to the store. Your mom is still working."

"Are you going to stay with us?" she asked.

He shook his head. "No, I have to go to work at the lodge.

I make music there for everyone. Remember? Say thank you to Miss Kirby."

"Kisses! I want kisses," Regan said, reaching for Hailey, her brown eyes shining.

Hailey came close enough for Regan to kiss her.

Hailey closed her eyes as Regan planted a kiss on her cheek, wondering how it would feel if Nick did the same. She inhaled the smell of his lemony after-shave and sighed as he stepped away. They'd talked as friends about books, the weather and such, but that was as far as it went.

"Okay, then. Regan will see you next time," said Nick in his deep sexy voice. He started to leave and turned back to her. "I did as you suggested and wrote to Lee Merriweather. I got an email back from her stating she'd be happy to consider my creating a couple of children's songs to go with her books."

"How nice," she replied with a smile, trying not to give herself away. "I think it's a great idea."

Nick shook his head. "There's something about those stories of hers. They're special. Because Regan loves them so much, I swear I've read each book of hers about a hundred times, and every time I'm reminded of something in my own childhood. Weird, huh?"

"Maybe. But I'm sure it would make her happy to hear that." Hailey's heart sang. His kind words made all the hard work, all the long hours of writing and illustrating a children's book worthwhile.

"Well, I guess I'd better go." Still holding Regan in his arms, he walked out of the library.

Hailey sighed again. Lee Merriweather was more real to Nick than she was. Didn't he remember meeting her as a young girl? The sweet way he'd knelt down to say hi was something she'd never forget. She'd been crushing on Nick since she was a kid.

Back then, she'd been a lot shyer, a lot quieter. Growing

up, her thick eyeglasses and strawberry-blond hair that would never cooperate didn't help. Everyone in her family told her she was adorable, a little pixie, and though she loved them for it, she knew better. Just before she entered high school, they all surprised her with Lasik surgery. It was the sweetest, best gift she could've imagined, a chance to do without her hated glasses. At the time, she couldn't stop crying at their kindness. The memory still brought tears to her eyes.

In her books, Charlie, too, wore eyeglasses. No coincidence.

Karen Peterson, the head librarian, walked over to Hailey. "I'm so sorry about Alissa's broken engagement. She deserves much better treatment than that."

"Yes, I think so too. My family is going to go ahead with their plans to stay at the lodge through Christmas to New Year's Day. I think it'll be good for all of us."

"Such a sweet family you have, Hailey," Karen said, beaming at her. "Maddie was so lucky to find you four girls."

"No," Hailey said firmly. "We girls are the lucky ones." She'd loved going from somebody no one wanted to one of the Kirby girls.

"Well, enjoy yourselves. And when you come back, be ready to go to work. I'll have a hard time explaining to the little ones why their marvelous Miss Kirby is away. Thank goodness our volunteers are willing to step in to give you the time off."

"The volunteers are wonderful. I can't thank them enough." Living in a small town like Granite Ridge had its advantages. The idea of supporting one another was a part of it.

❄

After Karen left, Hailey quickly wrote down instructions for the volunteers and mentioned a couple of books they might like to read aloud to the children. Every time she discovered a new book by a fellow author, she was thrilled to introduce it to the children. In some ways, it reminded her of her first night at her mother's house when she was a frightened little girl of eight. The story her mother read to her and Alissa was still one of her favorites. Who could resist saying goodnight to the moon?

With everything prepped at the library, Hailey bundled up, said goodbye to Karen, and headed out the door. Before going home to her condo, she had one errand to make. Hensley's Sweet Shoppe made the best chocolate-coated, caramel kisses ever. Those special holiday sweets were one of the first things her sisters asked for whenever they came home to visit. She planned to surprise them with a big box of the candy.

The frosty air outside took her breath away and nipped at her nose. But Hailey didn't mind. It was part of the charm of the season. Absorbing the bright colors of the lights and the holiday displays in the shop windows, she hurried along the street.

Hensley's Sweet Shoppe had a delightful, old-fashioned look to it with large paned-glass windows covering most of the front of the store on either side of the bright-red front door. The humidity of the indoor air had coated the windows with a frosty look that made the store even more inviting.

Hailey stepped inside, inhaled the enticing, sugary aroma, and grinned. Though she was careful about eating too many, she loved her sweets.

"Hey, Hailey! I've got your order for Christmas Kisses all ready for you," said Stacy, smiling at her, her hazel eyes agleam. She was all but hidden behind a starched, white apron. Her hair was covered by a pink baseball cap she wore to work in, but it couldn't hide a brown curl that trailed out from under it.

"Thanks!" said Hailey. "They're the best."

"By the way, I appreciate your including Regan in story time," Stacy said. "I know she's a little young to be there without me sitting with her, but it means the world to her to be able to be with the other kids to listen to you."

"No problem. I adore her. Regan is better behaved than some of the older kids, and she genuinely loves the stories. That means a lot."

"Regan and Nick both love to read." Stacy shook her head. "I swear, if Nick ever had the chance to meet the author of those Charlie books, he'd fall in love with her. He thinks she must be the most wonderful woman in the world."

"Really?" Hailey couldn't hold back her surprise.

Stacy nodded. "Oh, yeah. He hasn't told me too much about his time away playing guitar in his band, but he's one disillusioned guy about women. Apparently, they fell all over him because of his fame and so-called fortune. After being cheated out of a lot of money by his agent and with Mom's death, Nick was more than ready to come back to Granite Ridge to help me. Nick and I have promised to honor Mom's wishes to keep the candy store going. Thank goodness because that lying, cheating, scumbag ex of mine left me high and dry."

Stacy, as chatty as her mother had been, continued. "Yeah, underneath all the glamour, Nick is a quiet man who loves music and is content sharing it with others in a whole new way at the lodge." She winked. "I can't believe Stevie's younger sister has grown into such a beauty. You were always so shy, so hidden behind those glasses of yours. But you were adorable, Hailey. I remember all too well how you and those dogs of yours followed your sisters and me around for a bit."

Hailey laughed. Another part of living in a small town

meant your past was bound to nip you in the behind from time to time. "About the box of caramels?"

"Ah yes," said Stacy. "Here they are."

Hailey paid for the candy and waved goodbye. "Happy Holidays, Stacy. Give Regan a hug and a kiss for me."

"Will do. She's with the sitter, but I'll tell her. Best to all of you Kirbys."

A warm feeling kept the chill of the air away as Hailey hurried back to the library to get her car. She gripped the box of candy kisses in her hand. Kisses both real and imagined had been part of her life as a Kirby since the time her new mother gave her a stuffed dog to help make her feel more comfortable in her new home. At the suggestion of one of her sisters, she'd named that little, soft dog Charlie Brown. Other, real dogs followed.

In time, Hailey hoped to have a family of her own, complete with dogs. But in order to make that happen, she needed to find the right man.

Want to read more? Click here to download Christmas Kisses, Book Two in the Soul Sisters at Cedar Mountain Lodge Series.

ABOUT VIOLET HOWE

Violet Howe lives in Florida with her husband and three adorable but spoiled dogs. When she's not writing, Violet is usually watching movies, reading, or planning her next travel adventure. She believes in happily ever afters, love conquering all, humor being essential to life, and pizza being a necessity.

All of Violet's books explore the many facets of women's relationships—the romantic ones as well as those with friends and family. Depending on which title you choose, you might also find a mystery, an element of suspense, or a ghost or two. To learn more about Violet's books, visit www.violethowe.com.

Violet hopes you've enjoyed meeting Maddie, and if you'd like to spend more time with Maddie, Claire, and the four

Soul Sisters as they celebrate the holidays together fifteen years after their first, then check out Christmas Hope, Book Four of the Soul Sisters at Cedar Mountain Lodge Series.

ABOUT TAMMY L. GRACE

Tammy L. Grace is a *USA Today* Bestselling and award-winning author who entertains readers with perfect escapes, unforgettable characters, and binge-worthy series. She writes women's fiction, whodunit mysteries, and sweet Christmas stories. She is a huge fan of dogs and includes furry companions in all of her books and has published two dog-centric novels for Bookouture under her pen name, Casey Wilson.

When Tammy isn't working on ideas for a novel, she's spending time with family and friends or supporting her addiction to books and chocolate. She and her husband make their home in Nevada and have one grown son and a spoiled golden retriever. To learn more about Tammy's books, visit www.tammylgrace.com.

Tammy hopes you've enjoyed meeting Jo, and if you'd

like to spend more time with her, Maddie, and Jo's three Soul Sisters as they celebrate the holidays together fifteen years after their first, then check out her book, Christmas Wishes, Book Three of the Soul Sisters at Cedar Mountain Lodge Series.

ABOUT EV BISHOP

Ev Bishop is a *USA Today* bestselling author, best known for her small-town contemporary romance series, River's Sigh B & B. Readers describe her books as stories "full of humor, love and wisdom," set in places "where breathtaking scenery and the magic of love are the best medicine for the soul."

When Ev's nose isn't in a book or her fingers aren't on her keyboard, you'll find her with her family and dogs or playing outside, usually at the lake or in an overgrown garden somewhere.

She hopes you loved Stevie Fox as much as she does and that you'll catch up with her, Maddie, and the other three soul sisters, fifteen years after becoming a family, in Christmas Dreams, Book Five in the Soul Sisters at Cedar Mountain Lodge Series.

ABOUT TESS THOMPSON

USA Today Bestselling author Tess Thompson writes small-town romances and historical romance. She started her writing career in fourth grade when she wrote a story about an orphan who opened a pizza restaurant. Oddly enough, her first novel, "Riversong" is about an adult orphan who opens a restaurant. Clearly, she's been obsessed with food and words for a long time now.

With a degree from the University of Southern California in theatre, she's spent her adult life studying story, word craft, and character. Since 2011, she's published 25 novels and 6 novellas. Most days she spends at her desk chasing her daily word count or rewriting a terrible first draft.

She currently lives in a suburb of Seattle, Washington with her husband, the hero of her own love story, and their Brady Bunch clan of two sons, two daughters and five cats. Yes, that's four kids and five cats.

If you'd like to read the rest of Alissa's story, click here to download Christmas Rings, Book Five of the Soul Sisters at Cedar Mountain Lodge Series.

Tess loves to hear from you. Drop her a line at tess@tthompsonwrites.com or visit her website at https://tesswrites.com/

ABOUT JUDITH KEIM

Judith Keim enjoyed her childhood and young-adult years in Elmira, New York, and now makes her home in Boise, Idaho, with her husband and their two dachshunds, Winston and Wally, and other members of her family.

While growing up, she was drawn to the idea of writing stories from a young age. Books were always present, being read, ready to go back to the library, or about to be discovered. All in her family shared information from the books in general conversation, giving them a wealth of knowledge and vivid imaginations.

A hybrid author who both has a publisher and self-publishes, Ms. Keim writes heart-warming novels about women who face unexpected challenges, meet them with strength, and find love and happiness along the way. Her best-selling books are based, in part, on many of the places she's lived or visited and on the interesting people she's met, creating believable characters and realistic settings her many loyal readers love. Ms. Keim loves to hear from her readers and appreciates their enthusiasm for her stories.

Check out her website to learn more about her and her books, listen to samples of her audio books, and to contact her. Here is the link: https://www.judithkeim.com

Newsletters are sent on a regular, but not too often, schedule. You won't want to miss out on the latest news, win a prize, and meet other authors too. To sign up for her newsletter, go here: http://eepurl.com/bZ0ICX

Judith hopes you loved Hailey's story, and will spend more time with her mother, Maddie, her grandmother Claire, and her three sisters—Jo, Stevie, and Alissa by ordering all the books in this very special holiday series. Simply click here for a copy of Christmas Kisses, Book Two in the Soul Sisters at Cedar Mountain Lodge Series.

Made in United States
North Haven, CT
08 November 2022

26402940R00054